THE CHANGELING

The Changeling

A romance: the first in the Goblins and Cheese sequence.

Juniper Butterworth

Other works from this author

Writing as Sharon J. Gochenour

Monsters: A Retelling of Beauty and the Beast

The Threads Quartet
The Golden City
The Golden Empress (coming soon)

Table of Contents

PART ONE

When Taryn let the axe fall to the ground, all that was left was devastation. A stronger person could have swung the weapon high enough to reach the holiest carvings at the top of the shrine, the many-winged and wheel-eyed angels. Someone who had been trained in war, logging, or, indeed, in cabinet-making, could have found the structural joints and brought the whole thing crashing to the ground.

A woman as angry at one singular person as Taryn would have done exactly as she did: gone down the row of age-blackened figures depicting the king's lineage, cutting off the head of each king, queen, and ultimately each horse-lord, smashing their beautifully-carved, spindly limbs to matchsticks.

The king himself had arrived to watch the final, most damning act, as Taryn wrenched the seated figure of his mother from where it sat, looking sideways over the hall, and threw it to the flagstones. The neck broke immediately, and she made short work of the rest of it, the axe ringing as it cleaved through the wood and into the stone.

Only when the axe came to rest at her feet did he stride forward and yank it from her grip.

"You little monster," he said, his voice low, reasonable, furious.

"Send me home," Taryn said.

"I will not."

"Send me home."

"I cannot," he said flatly, and Taryn flew at him, her mind a sticky, opaque cloud of despair. She couldn't have said what she meant to do—whether she meant to seize the axe or pull the long knife from his belt or scratch his eyes out, or—or—

But the king seized her wrists in his brown hands and held her away from him. "Kandar," he said over his shoulder, his voice echoing against the far wall. Taryn saw now that a cluster of his horsemen stood in the shadows there, their eyes wide and their mouths shut tight. She felt her stomach clench and drop as Kandar stood forward. He did not meet her eyes.

"My lord," he said.

"Prepare Lilith."

Taryn jerked violently, but his hands clenched, and she could not pull free as he dragged her away from the shrine.

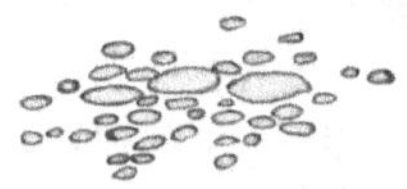

When the goblin king had stepped into the court of Taryn's father, he had been a slice of darkness through the color and sparkle. He wore no flashing cape nor ruffled collar nor gilded mask. The other fairies turned their faces away when they noticed him, and even the most terrible among them—the chimera and the sphinx chained to the walls on either sides of the throne, the redcaps skewered in grimacing positions among the topiary lining the walls, the harpy on her perch in the gallery—shifted uneasily.

Oberon himself— her father's name was not Oberon, except that name had always sat upon the throne, and now that was his place, so that must be his name as well—had made himself over all in silver, with a dozen pairs of shining wings exploding from his back and a shifting, glimmering train that draped to the ground between them. In the normal way of things he was a small, hunched, insect-like person, with hard, clawed hands and a mouth that tended to go sideways, but he had made himself magnanimous and resplendent for this night.

He made Taryn resplendent too, stretching her limbs and neck longer, making her hair shine with strange colors, tugging at her pupils and her irises until they were slitted and golden like a cat's. Her skin and bones ached, and she smiled her best mysterious smile. She loved her father, and she wanted him to love her. She knew he found the arch of her nose indelicate, her thick black hair and heavy black eyebrows coarse, and the thick flesh of her arms and chest and thighs repulsive, and she tried to forgive him changing her to look better, more lovable.

She vaguely knew there had been another daughter, a better daughter, before; that daughter could change her own face and her own hair. She could make Oberon laugh, not only in contempt, but at her clever words and wicked tricks.

Taryn thought of very little except pleasing her father, or at least—she hadn't—

The goblin king was a slice of darkness through the noise and brilliance, and all the fairies turned their faces from him; but the moment he stepped into her view she could look at nothing and no one else. He was very tall. His face hooked into a half-smile, deepening the lines around his black eyes and wide mouth. In the court of Oberon he wore tusks in his lower jaw and claws on all his fingers and toes, but it was easy enough to see that these could be shed if he wished to pass unnoticed through the shadows.

He walked to the edge of Oberon's dais, without a single fairy raising a hand or wing to stop him.

"Bug-lord," he said, and a little panicked murmur ran around the crowded court, before their conversations continued, faster, at a higher pitch, as though they could ignore the goblin king out of he room. The sphinx clicked her tongue, and the harpy muttered.

"Bug-lord," the goblin king repeated. He was tall enough to look Oberon in the eye as he sat on his throne. "I made you a promise, but I have not kept it."

He looked at Taryn, then, with his eyes black to the very edges, and she went very still and did not look away. She felt like she was dropping down into a very deep well, a well that was so deep that it opened up into sky and stars on the other end.

"More wine!" Oberon yelled, clicking and jingling his silver wings. He, too, refused to let his eyes touch the goblin king. "More beer! Bring in the dancers!"

"I promised to return to take your daughter, who I will make my queen," the goblin king said, in a voice that made all of Taryn's bones shake.

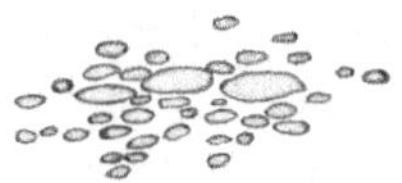

Lilith had six legs and hooves of razor-sharp iron. Her four eyes blazed red, and smoke curled from her nostrils. She was the only one of the king's horses who would carry Taryn, reeking of fairy magic as she did. The king threw her up into the saddle and mounted behind her, one hand resting against the pommel, the other arm banded tight around her waist. Lilith needed no reins to guide her.

They rode away from the castle on the way that went up the hill, crossing the high bog that stretched for days and days into the gray distance.

At first Taryn tried to struggle away from the king. If she could twist from his grip, she could throw herself off the road into the strange, stinking peat. There were paths that slipped between the pools and stands of bracken in any bog which led into Oberon's lands, and deep meres that had doors into his palace at their bottoms. This she knew from humans she had met in his court who had lost their way.

But the king's arm never loosened, and Lilith's teeth-rattling pace never slackened. Her hooves cracked into the ground like a great chain being snapped across the dirt again and again. The land grew dark around them, until Taryn could see nothing at all but the faint, reflected red glow from Lilith's eyes on the fabric covering her husband's chest, and hear nothing except the clattering of iron hooves and his furious breathing. Sometimes she thought she heard him whispering over her head; but surely that was the rushing of the wind around them.

The sky lightened and darkened and lightened again, and the bog rolled by them in swathes of green and gray. Lilith ran on. Taryn, who had never slept in the court of her father, fell into a doze, curled against the king.

On the fourth or fifth day the path went down at steep slope, and they rode out of a bog into a dark forest. The smell of pine was so sharp that Taryn woke fully for a moment and looked around her. The trees interlaced tightly overhead, and only a glimmer of sunshine made its way to the floor. There was no longer any road. Lilith ran over a carpet of dull red needles, snaking between trees and occasionally trampling bushes.

Time passed strangely on the bog, but it passed yet more strangely under the trees, where it was always shadowy. The tiny bits of light that reached them could have been the moon or the sun or the electricity of a storm; it was impossible to say. Every once in a great while, a cry echoed under the branches. Taryn dug her fingers into the king's arm and wondered if they had run back into Oberon's domain after all. But it was too gray for that, and there were no sparkling eyes at the back of the darkness all around them.

The king pulled Lilith to a halt in front of a tree that would have filled his whole hall from throne to arched entrance with its trunk and shaded the whole of his castle with its outstretched branches. Acorns littered the ground below it. Taryn came abruptly to appreciate these with her backside, as the king lifted her from the saddle and dropped her to the earth. She landed with a stunned thud, sending leaves and acorns swirling and spinning away from her.

The king looked down at her and pressed his lips together as though he would say something. Instead he set his knee against Lilith's shoulder. The mare turned her nose away from Taryn, sliding through a gap between two bowed hemlocks. Taryn heard the muffled sounds of hoofbeats for a minute, before she was left utterly alone in the wood.

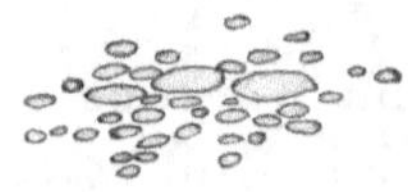

Taryn could not remember passing from fairy lands into the goblin kingdom. She had let the king take her hand, and at his gesture she stood up from the pouf where she sat just to the side of her father's feet. Even when she was not stretched out by magic, Taryn was much taller than Oberon, and when she stood on the dais her eyes were level with the goblin king's.

He smiled in a secret way that she recognized—but underneath the smile was something peculiar which she did not. It was that strangeness, perhaps, that she followed without hesitation, allowing the king to wrap his hands around her waist and lift her down from the dais. She could feel his fingers through her dress. She could not take her eyes away from his. He twined his large hand around hers and pulled her through the hall, his face hungry and just a bit hopeful.

The fairy courtiers and nobles parted ways for him just as quickly as before, without commenting or even seeming to notice that he took their lord's daughter away from him.

The goblin king tugged her through one of the arches that supported the harpy's gallery and around the corner, where he opened a door that had not been there before.

New doors opened into and out of Oberon's court at a cough or a whisper, mostly leading from one part of his palace into another, but sometimes crossing into another fairy's hill or one of any number of enchanted woods. This door had not been any different than any of those doors. They walked close together, her hand in his, through a room filled with gold vessels, and then a hall draped in jeweled fabrics, and then a low, wet cave that dripped and hissed. In the cave, Taryn felt the pad of the goblin king's thumb press into the center of her palm and trace a small circle. She stopped, uncertain, and he glanced back at her. She saw that his eyes had gone from purest black to a many-hued brown, amber and walnut and clay all glowing together.

They walked on, and somewhere along the way they passed

from where her father held power to where *he* did. The ground stopped emitting its own light, and objects stopped moving once they were out of her peripheral vision. Everything grew duller and more solid. They walked out of a narrow dark hallway filled with unseeable objects into dull twilight. They came to the top of a stony crag, and above them a hard white light had begun to pierce the blue-gray sky. On a higher, rockier hill just ahead, a blackened castle stood, partly ruined. When Taryn turned back, the narrow dark hallway had gone, and a gray moor spread in all directions where it had been. When she looked past the castle, the land softened into a bog.

"This, you will be queen of," the king said. "If you choose."

It was not quite a question.

Taryn stared up at the blackened castle, and then she looked at the tall brown figure next to her. He was, she suddenly understood, very beautiful, with a wide face, big nose, glowing eyes, and that half-hooked smile; his body was put together like it had been formed by someone who loved him deeply. He had drawn his own shadow so tightly about him in Oberon's court that he had been hard to see at all. When they had come out onto the hill, the shadow had dropped to the ground, and now he stood in his own glory.

Taryn's skin and bones hurt, worse than they had before. They often did after a ball when Oberon had changed her into something different, something more magnificent and interesting, as they slid over each other and reknitted themselves in what they had been. But now her gut and her chest clenched as well, as she looked at the beautiful king and what he offered.

"I will," she said.

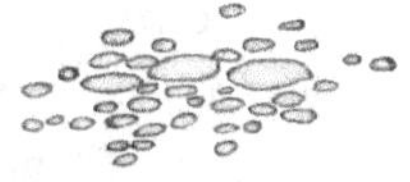

Taryn sat in the acorns for a long time, feeling hurt and a little stupid. She hadn't really been able to think since she had picked up the axe to destroy the shrine. She had been so angry and then—

if she were honest with herself—so bewildered and afraid, that she had not been able to put together what the king meant to do.

It seemed he had meant to abandon her in a forest.

Maybe he thought it was fitting punishment for destroying the icon of his mother, Taryn thought, getting to her feet. Her tailbone felt bruised, and several acorns dropped slowly from where they'd hooked themselves into the back of her dress. Most humiliatingly, her stomach squalled.

She had never felt hunger when she lived in her father's palace, Taryn thought automatically, and flinched. If she had destroyed one of Oberon's things with an axe, even a small thing for which he cared little, he would have poured hot coals into a box and locked her inside of it.

That knowledge fought with the terrible anger she felt toward the king, her husband. Her stomach twisted against itself. Rather than listen to it in silent misery, Taryn walked around to the other side of the tree.

The forest looked exactly the same on that side, but when she completed her circuit the two hemlocks where Lilith had made her exit had both disappeared. Taryn sighed. The acorns were still there, and she wondered briefly if she could eat them. If this were in fairy lands, she'd then be obliged to the tree for a thousand years, but the oak didn't feel sentient.

She made another circuit of the tree. This time when she passed the acorns, a maple sapling with brilliantly red, out-of-season leaves stood where the hemlocks had been.

Taryn narrowed her eyes and put her hands on her hips. She put her back to the tree and walked directly toward the sapling.

Whatever door or portal was there fizzed softly as she walked through it, and suddenly she was no longer in a dark, gray forest, but a different wood altogether, this one older and browner and filled with light. Undergrowth, blackberry brambles and currant canes and other scrubby things she could not name, tumbled and twined around every tree. All had green, hoary lichen growing on only one side of their trunks, unlike the black, slimy bark of the forest where the king had left her.

For lack of a better choice, Taryn faced the lichen and

started walking.

The forest heard her footsteps and shifted around her, making some paths longer and others shorter, pushing some places farther away and pulling one, particularly, very close.

The ground rose, enough that Taryn had to scramble over several large roots and pull herself up with the help of clumps of grass and low-hanging branches. At the top of the rise, she stopped.

She had never seen a witch-fence before, but knew immediately she was looking at one now. It was waist-high, woven of willow and hawthorn branches, with hanks of dirty wool tied around certain sections. It buzzed with a sound like a hornet trapped under a glass, though no part of it moved. When Taryn stepped closer, the buzzing intensified, and she saw that from each hank of wool hung a small, crude basket.

Curiosity drove her closer yet, and she peered into the nearest one. Inside was a chunk of brown-gray hair, still attached to the piece of skin it had grown from.

In the next basket was a finger.

Taryn drew back hastily. She looked down the length of the witch-fence and saw that every so often, the basket was replaced by a skull, wrapped in thin twine and tied tight against the snaking willows.

It was a powerful bit of magic. Taryn doubted that even Oberon could have crossed the fence, let alone any of the more minor fairies. A small lump of fear curdled in her stomach at the thought of meeting whoever had made this thing.

The forest would not let her turn away from the fence; no matter how she spun she ended up walking alongside it.

"I suppose I will see the witch, then," she said aloud, and the forest, gratified, brought her to a place where the fence followed the ground down into a hollow and wrapped around two great rocks to make a gate that opened into a dark copse of trees. The lintel stone had toppled down from the top of the gate and now was a wide, smooth flagstone before the entrance.

Taryn knew about gates and invitations, and if the forest would have let her she would have walked backward into its branches. As it was, she sighed deeply, before clearing her throat and calling out.

"Hello? Is there anyone there?" And then, even though she did not want to, "May I come in?"

The response came almost immediately from an invisible presence somewhere on the other side of the gate. "Good day, traveler. What do you mean to do here?"

"I am lost," Taryn said automatically. She almost burst into tears when she realized that it was true. "I want to go home. I won't be long."

"Come in, then," said the voice, and she walked through the gate.

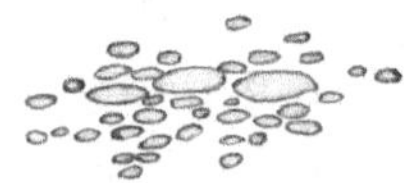

The goblin king led her up a narrow path to a small door in the side of the castle. When he pushed it open and she walked through into the courtyard, she saw that but for the heavy outer walls and a single, square tower, all inside lay in ruin. Thick vines had grown up over what once been a grand hall, and weeds fanned outward from all its windows. To her shock, horses milled about everywhere, animals of all colors and sizes and ages. Among them several large, round tents had been erected in the grassy bailey. One of animals, a blood bay, saw the king immediately and trotted toward him, ears flicked forward. When it snuffled his elbow, the king affectionately palmed its nose before turning it away from Taryn.

"I thought this was the goblin kingdom," she said, confused.

"My father's dwelling lies under this rock, and he and his household are the last of all goblins," the king said. "Once they were so many that they filled this castle and four more like it on the next hills, but now—" He shrugged. "When my mother made her camp here with her horses and her lords, he could not make her leave, or did not wish to."

He was already leading her toward the largest of the tents. This one had grand banners staked on all sides, each showing a yellow, snarling creature on a black field.

"My mother's standard," the king said. "A gryphon."

"That's not what a gryphon looks like," Taryn said skeptically, and he laughed and pulled her inside the tent.

The interior was draped heavily in rugs and skins. More banners lined the inside wall, and at the center a small brazier burned. Taryn realized she had been cold and getting colder since they had left Oberon's court, and her skin prickled all over as warmth returned to it.

Three tall, brown individuals sat on the ground around the brazier. One had tusks and was surely another goblin, though all three appeared very like the king. They all looked to him as he entered, smiling, until they saw Taryn, and then the smiles turned to incredulous laughs.

"What!"

"You've taken a queen after all!"

"She's very fine—"

"She doesn't look like—"

"That's not—"

"She isn't," the king said. "Now get out."

They rolled to their feet, laughing still and cursing, and each of them blinked both eyes at Taryn as they walked by her and ducked through the tent's flap.

The goblin king tied the flap shut. Taryn, looking around, was struck by how quiet the inside of the tent was, how muted the sounds from the outside were, how dim the light. It felt safe.

She pushed that thought away.

The king placed his hand on her lower back. "Will you be my wife?" he said, his voice very close to her ear.

"I will," Taryn said.

She knew what was coming, but it was strange with newness all the same. He produced a small blade and cut the ties that secured her dress. Tugging the garment open, he put his hand again on the bare skin of the small of her back. She shivered, hungry and hopeful, and turned against him, stretching out her hands uncertainly for the fastenings of his unfamiliar clothes. He laughed and guided her fingers to a brooch, which loosened his cape; two buttons, which opened his shirt-collar; and his belt.

Taryn knelt, thinking of certain things she had been shown to do by certain courtiers. This seemed like an easy way to please a beautiful king. She wanted very much for him to be pleased with her, for him to keep looking at her with the same strange, delighted look, as though he had stumbled upon a precious secret.

He looked down at her, his eyes greedy and very interested. She pulled his belt loose and then the cloth of his trousers, breathing a little laugh of relief when she saw that his parts were of the sort she knew more or less what to do with. That certainly hadn't always the case in fairy lands; there had been a few unexpected sets of claspers.

He, too, let out a small laugh when she put her mouth on him there, and then grew quiet as she sucked. After a few minutes, Taryn felt his hand at the back of his head, lacing his fingers through hair. She knew what that usually meant and took him deeper into her mouth, but instead he pulled her head back and away.

The king knelt with her, taking hold of her waist and then slouching back on the carpeted floor of the tent. She let herself be pulled down on top of him. He tugged at the neckline of her dress, which had been sewn for Oberon's preferred version of her and which was uncomfortably tight now that her body had fully reverted back to her normal shape. The little blade appeared again, and he slit the fabric down her front to her navel. Taryn inhaled sharply. She braced her hands on his shoulders and looked down at him, wondering what he would make of her body. Sometimes courtiers had been surprised, though she was not entirely sure by what.

The king did not seem surprised. He grinned up at her, and she found herself grinning down at him. He nuzzled his face between her breasts affectionately—Taryn thought of the horse nosing his elbow and laughed again—before pressing his teeth into one and sucking on the tip. He rolled her onto her side and worked his hands underneath the fabric of her dress as he pressed his mouth to one breast and then the other. He helped her wriggle her shoulders free from the short, too-slight sleeves of her dress, but when he had eased the fabric down to her wrists he didn't pull it free, but instead wrapped it firmly around her hands to pinion them at her back.

Taryn flushed and wriggled involuntarily. Her body felt warm all over, most particularly in the place between her legs. The king grinned more widely, as if to say, Isn't this a fun game we are playing? He bit her ear and then her neck, sucking a little bit on the same place before letting go. Taryn bit him back on the collarbone, feeling annoyed that she had not made him take off his shirt when she had undone his belt. She wished he would put his mouth back on her neck. She wished she could look at him.

He slid his hand down over her belly, hooking his thumb into her navel. She scowled at him and he laughed out loud. She inched closer and hissed in his ear, "Don't *tickle me.*"

His face pressed into her neck—yes, that was good, that felt lovely—and his hand continued downward. He touched her where she was soft, lightly, then lightly again. "Don't tickle you, like this?" His hand moved back and forth. "This?"

Taryn stilled, her eyes slipping out of focus as his fingertips circled. It was hard to remember to both inhale and exhale. She wanted to press closer to him, but her muscles didn't seem to be fully under her command. His right arm was wrapped tight around her side, holding her hands at her back; his other arm pressed against her front. She drew in a sharp breath when his fingers slid into her and the heel of his palm came to rest on the most sensitive bit. He started to rub.

Her breathing sped up as she pushed her hips into his hand again and again. Then she didn't breathe at all for a long minute and clenched her jaw, before slumping into the king's shoulder, her heart beating furiously in her ears.

He freed her wrists and rolled her onto her back. Taryn shoved at the tattered remains of her dress, still tight around her hips. The king kissed her neck and she wrapped one arm around his head to hold him there, wishing vaguely that she could manifest another hand to get this damned skirt off. She kissed his ear, his temple, just beside his crinkled eye. Again, he made short work of the fabric, though she couldn't see how he did it. He sat back, pressing her thighs wide with both hands, his fingers digging into her skin. Then he leaned forward again, settling firmly on top of her and catching one of her wrists in each hand.

Taryn closed her eyes and felt: the scratchiness of the rug on her back; each of his fingertips on the bones at the back of her hands; the solid weight of him stretching the insides of her thighs. She felt safe, protected, and she was too aroused and too tender to force that thought out of her head. Safe, safe.

She strained her face toward his, but he had lifted himself a little to rearrange himself to couple with her. When he pushed inside of her, she sucked in air hard through her nose. This bit was not something any of the courtiers had done, lest she get with a child that Oberon did not want.

It hurt, and when her eyes focused she realized the king was watching her face intently as he moved slowly over her. His gaze burned, and she closed her eyes again. He became still, waiting. After a few minutes, she was able to encourage him a little with her hips, and his rhythm increased. Taryn could feel her body beginning to quicken again, to pulse in time with his, but the feeling was too strange to rise to the point of breaking.

When he was done, he brought her face close to hers, lightly touching her cheekbones and her chin with the tip of his nose. She bit him lightly on the jaw.

"I would like to do that again," she whispered.

"There will be time," he said, his lips moving against her cheek.

The king produced a blanket from a box near the brazier and rolled her naked body up in it as though she were a bit of potato in a dumpling. Taryn, annoyed at this manhandling, opened her mouth to complain, then suddenly found herself asleep.

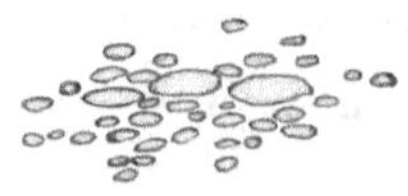

The forest changed again abruptly on the other side of the stone gate. The witch-fence must have had some sort of misdirection or illusion twined through its weft. What had looked like a foreboding copse of trees from the other side had transformed itself into a grassy meadow of oats and wheat and wildflowers, cranky apple-trees gnarling around raspberry canes and wild grapes in a hedge around the borders of the field. At the far boundary of the meadow stood an oak as massive as the one the king had left her under, a pile of rubble at its foot.

In the center of the meadow stood a person holding a large, half-full basket, looking at her inquisitively. This was clearly the witch. Taryn could smell the magic off them, something that anyone who survived longer than a week in Oberon's court could do. Besides that their arms were bare, displaying skin heavily tattooed with vines that shifted and flickered around peculiar diagrams. These made Taryn somewhat queasy, so she looked at the witch's face instead.

Their hair was clipped very short, but Taryn could see that it was brown with the beginnings of gray at the temples. She thought the witch had once been a pale, northern sort of person, but had spent so much time out-of-doors that they had been burnt quite brown. They had rounded features, a short nose and a rather weak chin, but a mouth that was used to smiling and eyes with crows' feet.

That last made Taryn feel terribly, inexplicably lonely, and she shook her head.

"Who are you?" she asked.

"I'm no one," the witch said, not unkindly. "Where are you going?"

"I—" Taryn caught her breath. "I want to go home," she said, but found that *home* was suddenly very hard to remember. It was sparkling lights and—and—great beasts, great horses—no, that last bit wasn't right—and there were tall knights, brown men and women—but no, that wasn't what she wanted—

"Are you doing this?" she demanded, tears in the corners of her eyes. "I can't think—"

"It's the wood," the witch said. "It gets in your way until you see what it wants to show you. Look." They shifted the basket to one hip and offered a hand to her. "Come inside and have something to eat. It will come back to you in a bit, if you let your mind go the way the forest asks you to."

"I've been doing nothing but that since I got here," Taryn

said bitterly, but she took the witch's wide, square hand and walked next to them toward the massive oak.

The pile of rubble resolved itself into a scrubby little house sunk into the roots of the tree. It was hard to see where the grass of the meadow became the roof and where the stones of the field became the walls. Two little steps led down to the low wooden door.

"I've been working on it for years now," the witch said proudly. "See!"

Inside another five stone steps went down along the wall to the floor of the single, large room. To their right a stone hearth loomed; to their left was a table and chairs of dark wood. A loft cut across the windowless back of the house. The low, dark space below it was filled with heavy crocks and barrels. Dried, rustling bundles hung densely from every rafter, and more stacks of jars lined all the walls. Taryn sneezed. The house was very dim, and the shadows moved.

"Sit," the witch said, gesturing to one of the chairs, and Taryn sat. The witch knelt at the hearth and clattered about with coals and irons, before getting to their feet and pulling a number of bundles from the rafters and pawing through a particularly enormous crock. They assembled a small iron rack and a lump of bread and several jars. She realized belatedly that they were making toast. She watched the tattoos on their muscled forearms shift as they worked and thought confused thoughts about bread and hands.

Taryn glanced upward, at the motes of dust spiraling down from the high, narrow windows. The forest did not seem inclined to let her consider home yet. Instead, she inhaled the scent of browning bread and brewing spices and swallowed hard.

After a minute the witch took down a tray and stacked many small pots on it, finally adding a large kettle and the toast rack. They brought this tray to the table and proceeded to assemble the most decadent toast that Taryn had ever seen: two huge slabs of brown bread, each smeared with a heaping spoon of butter, coated in honey, piled with white, creamy cheese, and finally spread with a thick layer of cooked fruit.

"Eat that, and I'll make you more," the witch said. Taryn started to the object, but they had already turned back to the hearth and started cutting more slices of bread.

She would scrape off the toppings and only eat a half-slice, she told herself. She wasn't a glutton. She was—she was a beautiful daughter—a beautiful daughter of *someone*—and she didn't *need* to eat. Besides—didn't food obligate her? Wouldn't she be bound to the witch in some way, if she fell under the spell of the toast?

Her stomach screamed and stabbed at her backbone. Taryn drew in a deep, shaky breath.

She ate both huge slices of toast, and two more dripping with butter and fruit, and then two more again with eggs and slices of hard sausage that the witch fried together in a great iron pan, and she drank the unfamiliar hot drink they made for her, heavy with cream and cinnamon. The witch continued to produce food from various crocks, looking at her with gentle amusement. Taryn ate until her belly ached with fullness.

"I reckon you were hungry enough, then," they said finally, leaning against the back of the other chair.

"I—" Taryn started, her face going red. "I only—"

"It's not a bother to me," the witch said, still kind. "I've four cows and six goats in the other field, and five of those milking."

"I didn't mean—" Taryn shook her head, suddenly very tired.

"I wouldn't have offered if I didn't mean it," they said briskly. "You'll have a nap now, and then maybe when you wake you'll have sorted things out in your head."

They showed Taryn the ladder cleverly carved into the wooden support of the loft, and after a token resistance she climbed up into the nest of quilts and featherbeds. Her body felt like she had not slept in at least a week, and she had barely made a small space beneath the mound of coverlets before she was deeply asleep.

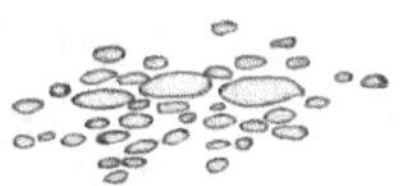

The king's castle overwhelmed Taryn. It was small, four hundred paces from one outer wall across to the bailey to the other, and nothing moved. There were a set number of people who came and went, and she was expected to know all their names. Many of them were cousins to the king—real cousins, children of his mother's sisters or her mother's sisters. In Oberon's palace "cousin" was a word with no particular meaning, used as readily for a stranger as the strange, shadowy folk she suspected were her father's actual kin.

She got on the wrong side of one of the goblin cousins immediately. He came into the big tent sometime after the king had left her there rolled in a blanket.

She had spent several hours in a shallow doze, dreaming hazy, anxious dreams. The sounds of someone opening boxes, taking things out, and closing other boxes brought her fully awake and her eyes open. A big goblin, tusks, claws, ears, and head-crest all on display, crouched on the other side of the brazier, his face down in a carved chest.

Taryn propped herself up on her elbow and spoke in a clear voice. "I want breakfast and a bath."

The goblin stopped and stared at her. His eyes were as multifaceted as the king's, in shades of yellow, gold, and amber.

In Oberon's palace, Taryn thought, this would be a test, to see if she was brave enough to demand that her authority be respected. She took a deep breath. "Go and get them for me."

The goblin sat back on his heels, still staring at her, then rose to his feet.

That went well, Taryn thought, feeling rather smug. The smug feeling lasted until the goblin returned with a pitcher of cold water, which he dumped over her head, and a piece of dry bread, which he threw on the sopping rug next to her.

Taryn gasped and screamed. It suddenly struck her that she was alone, without even clothes that she could call her own, in a place where she knew no one and had no friends.

Not, she thought bleakly, that she had friends in her father's court.

The goblin went back to digging through the trunk. Taryn felt panic rising in her chest. If she didn't get control now, what would become of her? Would the goblin king's household assume she could be bullied, forced to do as they liked? She had seen this happen to guests of Oberon, fosters or hostages from other hills who were not up to fighting the viciousness of his servants and the machinations of his nobles. Some of them disappeared; some of them merely faded into obscurity and humiliation.

She would not let that happen to her.

Taryn sat all the way up, arranging the wet blanket around herself with as much dignity as she could manage. "The king is my husband," she said. "I am your queen."

He did not look up. "I am your equal," he said, coldly. "Go soak your head."

Later, she would find out that this was Kandar, the only son of the old queen's most beloved sister, fostered with the king as a brother since birth—and perhaps the only person in the world who did not think twice about entering the king's tent without an invitation and rifling through his things. Many of the objects in the boxes and trunks were gifts Kandar himself had bestowed upon the king, treasures secured on long and strange adventures taken together, when his mother were still alive, and apart, after she had died and her son had bowed his head under the twined crowns of goblin and horse-lord.

Taryn, shivering in her blanket, knew none of this.

"I will make sure the king knows of your rudeness," she said, trying to keep the fury and fear out of her voice.

"Go ahead and tell him," the goblin said. "He's in the hall." He shook out a long piece of embroidery from the trunk, one sewn all over with luminous stones.

Taryn bit back an angry response and rose to her feet. She glanced about desperately for something she could wear. Going before the king in a blanket would surely only reinforce her weak position here. Why hadn't he left her any clothes? Did he *want* her to be at a disadvantage? Was this another test?

She shoved open the lid of the box where the king had taken the blanket and dug desperately. It was filled with coverlets and flat textiles with strange patterns and textures, but near the bottom she found a robe of smooth, fine wool, dyed in a wavy pattern. It was very large, and even when she wrapped another bit of fabric tightly around her midsection it gaped at the chest and dragged behind her on the ground.

Taryn thought the other goblin stopped to watch her push the tent flap open and step outside, but she refused to look behind her.

Outside it was still early in the morning, the light as hard and white as it had been the day before. Taryn took a moment to get her bearings, looking nervously at the three horses grazing untethered next to the tent. Two of them went on ignoring her, but the third lifted its head and eyed her suspiciously.

She strode toward the square tower at the far end of the bailey, flinching as the wet, cold grass squelched under her feet. The ground was soft, and it was not easy to avoid the muddy dents in the ground left by horse-hooves.

Two goblins stood either side of the arched entrance to the tower. Each held a long spear with a silver blade and a had a long, curved sword belted at their waist. They did not try to stop Taryn when she walked past them, nor did they come running after her when she pushed open the great door between them.

The chamber beyond was nothing like Oberon's throne room. For one, there was no throne. Occupying the center of the space was a multi-tiered wooden—*thing*—nearly twice her height, carved all over with strange figures and animals and designs. But for a few of the carvings on the lowest level, the wood was dark with age. Light poured down from above to illuminate the massive wooden horses holding up each of the four corners. When Taryn looked up she found that the hall had no proper roof but a huge piece of waxed canvas stretched from wall to wall.

She looked down in alarm. The hall was otherwise bare.

"This is Taryn," the king's voice said. "She is my queen, who I have claimed from the fairy court."

He walked around the corner of the shrine, followed by two other individuals. Taryn looked at them carefully, but she didn't think they were goblins, or not quite. An assortment of wire-haired hounds trailed behind one, some as tall as her waist.

"Have you said vows?" this figure asked, the question divided equally between her and the king.

"Not yet," the king said, a note of chagrin in his voice. "There were other matters to be attended to."

His eyes flicked toward Taryn and held her gaze. She did not blush, but she thought of her shredded dress and stood up very straight.

"Then they must be done immediately," said the dog-attended figure. "Before the shrine, so all the queens and horselords may witness it."

"And on the stone, so all the kings and masons may witness it," added the other, whose brow was creased in a rather quizzical expression.

They both turned to stare at Taryn, who wished very much that she had spent longer looking for something suitable to wear among the king's possessions.

"Very well," she said stiffly. "What must I pledge?"

"Many things, in the languages of our mothers and fathers both," the quizzical-looking one said.

"I will not vow something I do not understand."

"The vows must be said at once," the dog leader snapped. "You should not have been brought here before they were made sure."

"Surely there is time to translate them."

"They do not translate well," the quizzical-looking one said dryly. "They are understood in the taking."

They looked to the king, whose glowing eyes had returned to Taryn's.

"If I vow first," he said slowly, "that what is asked of you will bring you no harm nor sorrow, will you trust me and repeat what must be said?"

Taryn thought of the goblin in the tent and his pitcher of cold water and clenched her hands in the folds of the robe. "Will I be—" Would she be alone, set against all the rest of them, waiting always upon the favor of the king, as she had been on the whims of Oberon? "Will I be the first in your household?" she asked finally.

"You will be among equals in my household," the king said.

She swallowed hard, thinking of the horses, the goblins, the tents, the roofless hall, with a dim premonition of what life would like among them; dull and solid and unchangeable. She thought of the king's eyes, his hand on her back, his hand on other places on her body; and suddenly, horribly, she thought also of Oberon changing and stretching her flesh before a ball, squeezing her bones into beautiful, elegant shapes.

"I will trust you," she said to the hall, a little too loudly and a little too quickly, her eyes not quite focusing. "Vow to me, and I will pledge to you."

The king spoke his pledge, in a ringing voice that hummed in her blood. The dog-attended figure looked sharply from him to her and then to the shrine, before pronouncing a slow string of syllables which she repeated.

The syllables went on for a very long time, and as Taryn uttered them she felt a new, peculiar weight settle into her bones, as if they had been hollow up until this moment and were now being filled up with some heavy liquid. She thought at first she could tell the two languages apart, but as the vows went on them they twined together to make a new, sharper speech. The twining wrapped around her and down, into the dirt, through the soil and up again, into horse-bones, goblin-claws, tent-stakes, spear-hafts. The vows made a netting that tied her to the whole world, it seemed.

The last word shook the dust off the top tier of the shrine and made the stones of the hall jig against each other for a split second, before a quelling silence fell.

Before it could crush Taryn under its weight, the silence was broken again, by a cacophony of voices all around her. While she had spoken, dozens—hundreds?—of goblins and other horse-folk had filed into the hall, crushing close around her.

"Hail! Hail, Queen! Here is the Queen! Hail!"

The morning toast plate featured stewed beans, sliced, fried mushrooms of many sorts, poached eggs, strips of bacon streaky with fat, and a large quantity of brown sauce which, after a tentative taste, Taryn determined to be made from crushed nuts. All of this was layered on slices of bread that were as thickly slathered with butter and honey as the night before.

She ate three pieces before taking breath and a deep draft from the steaming mug at her elbow. It tasted of mint and elderflower.

The witch was sweeping the ashes out of the cold part of the hearth, humming tunelessly. They were very short and broad when viewed from the back, Taryn thought, sort of like a badger had stood up and put on trousers and a quilted jacket.

"What is your name?" the witch asked, without turning around.

Taryn, warm and full of toast, bit back the first syllable when she realized what she was doing. "What's yours?" she snapped.

"Ash," the witch said calmly. "Have you remembered what you're about, or will you be staying for lunch?"

Taryn stared down at the table. The truth she was looking for sat in the middle of her mind, like a great black boulder she could neither ignore nor roll away. It was obvious and yet unknowable. Thinking about it directly made the back of her skull ache. She suspected that whatever end she was on her way toward was something nasty, and she suddenly wanted to put it off as long as possible. Her thoughts, though, kept slipping back to the boulder, worrying the same question over and over. What was she *doing* here?

"I was—I was angry with someone," she said, and that sounded true, "someone I loved," and that was true too, but the last word tasted bitter.

"Did that person love you?" Ash asked.

Taryn rolled an answer around in her mouth and swallowed it. "Whatever I am to do, it is a fair return," she said sharply.

"Hm," they said. "Well, you can come out and help me weed the turnip bed, and if you figure it out by half past noon, I'll pack you a basket and you can be on your way."

Ash picked up the dishes and carried them outdoors to a large dry sink to wash in a pail of water. Taryn, suddenly embarrassed, put the bits of leftover food back in crocks, before going out to take the dried plates and cups and put them on a rack on the other side of the hearth.

Each of them took a large basket and a long, sharp stick and walked up the meadow behind the massive oak. Ash led Taryn through a thin line of young trees into another small clearing hedged around in dense hawthorns.

"I don't care for them, but the birds like the berries, and the pigs would be at the turnips otherwise," Ash said, jerking their chin at the bushes, pushing open a gate of dark wood. The hinges and latch pieces were all of iron, Taryn saw. The witch didn't have their magic from fairy blood, then. She poked the latch back into place with a stick she pulled from the hedge.

Inside the hedge grew several dozen rows of leafy fountain-like greens and another few dozen pale green orbs. While the first section was weedy, sunburnt, and bug-eaten, the cabbages were pristine spheres.

"Have you already weeded those?" Taryn asked, pointing.

Ash dug their stick into a clump of crab grass as though they hadn't heard. Taryn sniffed deeply. There was a low carpet of magic which bubbled up around each cabbage plant, with angry injunctions against insects and birds and rabbits woven throughout.

"Couldn't you just charm the whole garden, then?"

Ash flung the grass over the hedge and glanced back at Taryn. Their voice held a note of embarrassment. "The beets don't care for it. And I feel funny about trying skip out on the work."

"What about the cabbages?"

The witch narrowed their eyes at the other half of the garden. "I don't care what those smug bastards want."

Taryn laughed, and Ash looked up in surprise before smiling too.

She fell in beside the witch, stabbing her stick into the base of huge thistle. It didn't budge. "Have you always been in this wood?"

"Oh no. I had adventures and so forth." Ash came to Taryn's rescue, sliding their stick down next to the thistle's taproot so they could pincer it up together. "As people do when they're young."

"Do they?" Taryn asked, her heart a bit hollow. She tackled a buttonweed as tall as her waist.

"Well, some of them," they amended. "I expect I've been in the wood close on a decade—maybe longer. Time is a funny old thing in here."

"Where did you go adventuring?"

"A dozen kingdoms and more," Ash said, laughing. "I can't remember all of them, and I wouldn't if I could."

"The goblin kingdom?" Taryn asked, refusing to follow the question to its root.

"That's hardly an adventure now, is it? I've had great friends from the goblin kingdom. It's only an adventure if you don't know who or what you might find."

"What did you find, then, in those other kingdoms?"

The witch thought for a minute, and then told a story about a dragon with three heads and a vicious temper. When Taryn leaned on her stick and watched hungrily, they went on, telling another story about a dragon worshiped as a god, then another about a dragon that had transformed partway into a tree, then finally one about a dragon—or perhaps it had been a wyvern—who had chased all the workers out of a biscuit factory and brooded her eggs in a large pile of biscuit tins.

"I don't believe you," Taryn said.

"I'll show you one of the tins," Ash said. "I keep cinnamon sticks in it."

"Tell me another," Taryn said, remembering herself enough to angle the stick into a huge burdock.

Ash told more stories, some of them very grim and some of them very funny. They consistently featured a character they called the Prince, one or two of the Prince's wild cousins, and occasionally a mold-fairy named Slug. When half-past twelve came, they led Taryn out of the hedge and down to the house. She sat at the table and watched as the they flipped a great round mass of dough out of a crock into a iron pot, which they pushed with a poker into the hottest spot in a niche at the very back of the hearth. They served Taryn a dish of cold white cheese with sugared fruit preserves ladled over the top, followed by a stew of pork and onions and turnips.

"Don't you eat?" Taryn asked, blushing as she wiped a smear of peach from her cheek. After the morning of fighting with weeds, she'd been hungry enough to eat all the cheese and fruit and three bowls of soup.

Ash looked up from the crock into which they were packing some vegetables and thumped their thick torso with a sound like a drum. "Never fear." Then, kindly, "Do you want to come milk the beasts with me, or do you want a nap? They're out in a field a ways past the turnips."

Exhaustion crooned to Taryn from the marrow of every bone, and it embarrassed her so much that she sat bolt upright and glared at the witch. "I'm fine, thank you. I'll come with you."

The witch shrugged and nodded. Taryn knew she'd made a mistake when Ash loaded each of them down with a wooden yoke, a bucket hanging on each end. She found she could barely walk straight under the weight of the empty vessels.

"Here now," Ash said, tapping the underside of each bucket. Suddenly the yoke weighed barely anything at all.

"Do you do that with yours as well?" Taryn asked, starting up the hill after them.

"Do you really want to know?"

"No."

"Very good."

The goats and cows were in a field with no hedge around it, but a strong suggestion laid on the trees that the grass really did taste best where the sun shone brightest. A shadow in the trees caught Taryn's eye, and she turned to see a large spotted goat observing them from among the trees, perched on top of a downed pine.

"Goats are selectively impervious to magic," Ash said, following her gaze. "Especially Hender, there. She belonged to a sorcerer for a while."

"What happened to the sorcerer?"

Ash wiggled their eyebrows but said nothing. Taryn thought of the skulls on the witch-fence and wondered.

They unhooked a bit of wood from the end of their yoke

that Taryn realized was a sort of two-legged stool. The cows had looked up with interest as soon as Ash had come out of the trees, and now they'd formed a ring around the two of them, sniffing with their great wet noses. Their calves were even less polite, and one of them immediately grabbed a corner of Ash's jacket and sucked on it loudly. One goat reared on her hind legs, trying to knock a bucket off of Taryn's yoke with her horns; Ash elbowed the animal in the side and she stopped. Four or five or six kids—the number seemed to change every time Taryn tried to count—each no higher than her knees, periodically bounced out of the grass and ricocheted with tiny hooves off a shin or an ankle, bleating loudly.

Ash produced a bag from inside their quilted jacket, and the animals drew closer.

"Oats," they said, seeing Taryn's confused look.

They commenced a complicated ballet in which the bag of oats was always just out of reach for a variety of noses, while the four buckets were taken down and deftly filled with milk in turn. Ash showed Taryn how to balance on the stool, how to wipe down the teats with a cloth and accordion her fingers over them to pull the milk down. The udders of the cows and the goats were quite different, and Taryn could swear each animal turned around to watch her bemusedly as she tugged furiously at them.

Ash stood beside her, occasionally covering her hand with one of their own to correct how she held her fingers. Sometimes a tattoo would curl down their thumb when they did this, briefly becoming a leaf or a flower before flowing away again. Their chest pressed against her shoulder each time, quickly, before they pulled away. It was not a familiar gesture—Taryn remembered, dully, around the boulder in her mind, sparkling people who would not let go of her hand or stop kissing it, no matter what she said about it— but it was intimate. She felt embarrassed and then warm and then embarrassed again.

Even after the oats were gone, the goats rubbed their faces on Ash's trousers and presented the tops of their heads for scratching.

"It's the horns, you know," the witch said philosophically, rubbing the face of a nanny the color of polished wood. The goat leaned sleepily against their legs and stretched her face upward. "Horns are always itchy."

"I'll keep that in mind," Taryn said, eyeing the goat with some envy.

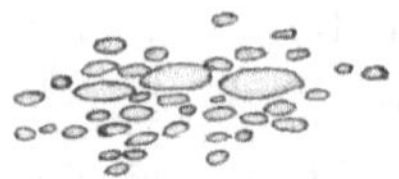

The king had several suits of clothes made for Taryn. These were not like any clothes she had ever worn before, loose trousers and shirts of brilliantly-dyed wool, held close to the body with embroidered vests and leg wraps.

Though all of the horse-folk and many of the goblins wore equally bright garb, she felt horribly conspicuous. With the notable exception of Kandar, who ignored her pointedly, the occupants of the castle were terribly interested in Taryn, and the scarlet vest and pantaloons and sky-blue shirt made her easy to find. The goblin knights wanted to know about her fighting skills; Taryn showed them what knifework she had and fired a few arrows with respectable accuracy into a target. Their wizard, the horse-lord with the dogs who had recited her vows to her, recognized that she'd used magic to pull the arrows in, and this led to a demonstration of what spells and castings she knew.

The king extracted her with good and resolute humor every evening from whatever knot of his relatives had twined around her. She ate with him and a few of his councilors and cousins in the great tent, plain meals of vegetables and herbs and only rarely venison or pork, and tried to understand their conversations. They sat cross-legged around a polished board with the dishes arrayed in a circle on its surface, each of them spooning stew onto pieces of bread in turn. To her surprise, they spoke mostly of human kingdoms, of human concerns and politics and trade. She could not remember her father ever mentioning the human world as more than a passing thought, usually in reference to some miserable hostage he had recently acquired.

After the dinner was eaten down to bare, greasy plates, the

king clapped his hands and pointed at the door. "Out," he said, pleasantly enough, and the councilors and the cousins went, snorting and chuckling to themselves.

Taryn did not know what to expect, those first few nights. Her first time with the king had been pleasurable, but it was maybe too much to expect that he pay her so much kindness again. A king, as she knew from her father, had limited attention, even for his favorites. She could imagine any number of indignities—any number of situations she could grit her teeth through, if necessary to remain queen—she was not a child and did not expect everything to be easy and gentle—

The king sipped from a goblet and watched her over its rim, his amusement showing in the crinkling around his eyes, until she grew annoyed, took the wine from him, and pushed him down onto the rugs.

In the mornings, the king sometimes left before she woke. When she asked, the cousins said that he rode out, but they either would not or could not say where. If she pushed too hard or asked too many questions, one of them would invariably disappear and reappear holding the halter of a horse. Didn't Taryn think she ought to learn to ride now?

This was an effective stop to the interrogation. The horses were as wary of Taryn as she was of them. Every mount brought within an arm's-length of the new queen stood stock-still, feet planted, ears back, whites showing around both eyes.

On days when the king was still there when she woke, the castle took on a strange character, one she could not recognize from Oberon's court. The fastidious respect of her father's courtiers, Taryn understood, was derived from the fear of being turned into a snail or trapped in an oak tree for a thousand years. The esteem that the goblin king's family and retainers bore him seemed to come from some other source, one that did not prevent his younger cousins from hurling themselves upon him when he emerged from his tent, his various aunties demanding he practice at swords or play chess with them, or the horses affectionately drooling down his tunics. None were so flippant nor as rude as Kandar, but none of them seemed wary of the king's anger, either.

Taryn hastily followed him from the tent, anxious to see what he saw and be seen as his consort. The king led her through the tents, commenting seemingly at random on things they passed: which cousins belonged to which aunties, who had done which bit of tent embroidery or carving of the decorative stakes, and the lineage of each and every horse. It was like and unlike the politics she knew from the fairy realms. There were as many names to remember—though a disproportionate number of them were attached to equines—and as many subtle signals to the history and allegiances of each of the cousins—though they all watched her with the same curious, distanced look. She could not discern any tensions or faultlines through which she could ingratiate herself.

The wizard, whose name was Ildar, was more talkative but less helpful. He spoke of magics, of worlds, of breaking-places and meeting-places. Taryn thought some of this had to do with the fairy realm, and she thought that on the days he vanished early in the morning, the goblin king was out wandering between different hills, doing. . . what?

Unsettled by this line of thinking, she began to plan a grand reception for Oberon to attend in the castle, at the head of the Fairy Hunt. They rode out only rarely, but when they did there was a great cacophony of horns and drums and singing, all of them mounted on unicorns, kelpies, pookas, and other fairies bespelled to look like horses. Oberon himself rode the chimera, the fire of its dragon head ensuring that no one crowded the king.

There would be a great table that crossed the bailey, Taryn thought, and at one end she and her king would sit, and at the other Oberon. They would lay out all the dishes before the fairies came, beautiful dishes—

The difficulty of what to serve made her pause. The goblins' food—bread and stew, stew and bread, boiled turnips and cabbages, occasionally a pot of rice with saffron pitched in—would not do for Oberon's fastidious tastes. She did not know how far the human kingdoms were from this domain or how long it would take the horse-folk to bring her back fine spices, dragonfruits and starfruits, veal calves, peacocks, small whales—it might be a matter of months, and what if some of it spoiled on the way? She steadfastly refused to consider whether any of the goblins would accept such commands from her. The logistical troubles were enough and far less terrifying.

She would have to bewitch the food, she decided, to make it more beautiful and savory and delicate. Her father might be impressed by her ingenuity, if nothing else. It was not a sort of magic she had tried before, but building illusions of other sorts had been a daily necessity before. She would get some bread, and she would practice.

The goblin king from that point on found her many evenings sequestered in his tent, her brow furrowed as she coaxed bread to taste like figs, dates, apricots; to become fluffy as meringue or creamy as pudding; to puff upward and form a crisp, barely-there crust that could be cracked with the tap of a spoon. It was easier to do if she had something of what the real thing was, so she stole spoonfuls of honey and oil from the tent where the foodstores were kept. When she was caught by Thalar, a goblin cousin so large that mounting a horse for him was more like stepping over a stile, he politely gave Taryn her own jars of honey and oil, and a very old clove of nutmeg as well.

As the weeks wore on, the king more and more often returned to the tent silent and pensive. When he found Taryn alone there, working steadily to turn a stale slice of bread and some sour berries into a tower of raspberry cream puffs in the shapes of clouds, he often did not fetch the cousins and councilors to eat dinner and confer with him. Instead he watched her spellcraft, his eyes thoughtful, before stepping outside to request a tray of food. She locked her shoulders, bracing for a sardonic question that never came. Oberon would certainly not have let her work so long on anything without demanding to know what was about and, once he knew, that she finish it more quickly, so that she might return to her attention to him.

Sometimes, if she woke in the night from unsteady dreams, she saw the shadow of the king move across the tent to the board where she had laid out her magic. He picked up her bespelled pieces of food and lifted them, one after the other, to his nose, inhaling deeply.

Taryn wondered uneasily how long her father would wait for an invitation to the goblin kingdom before he became offended and refused to come—or, worse yet, decided the offense was reason enough to cause havoc. A small, secret part of her worried that he would not remember her after she had been out of his sight for a week, but she shoved that part deep down into the shadows in her heart and refused to think about it.

When two months had passed, and Taryn had built and rebuilt an intricate ice-palace of spun sugar—made from honey and bits of sand; a roast stag with six antlers—made from a snared rabbit and birch twigs; a pie that burst into a vast bouquet of lilies and roses carved from roast tubers when it was sliced—made of hollowed-out loaf and some faintly moldy potatoes—to the point where she was quite sure they would last through a grand banquet, she spoke to the king.

"My lord," she said, one night after the cousins and councilors had left, when the two of them sat on across from each other on the rugs. "I would honor my esteemed father by inviting him to a wedding feast inside the castle."

The king, who had been easy and gentle and even kind, set his wine on the board and looked at her.

"No."

"Perhaps it is not a good time," Taryn said, her heart drumming in her ears. "When, my lord, would it be convenient to you to host my father?"

"Never," said the goblin king. "Oberon will never be welcome in my kingdom."

"Then when will I be allowed to visit him?"

"When I am dead and my body is crumbled to dust," he said.

"Oh," said Taryn. "I see." Her heart felt like it had frozen in her chest.

She closed her mouth and laid down on the rugs.

In the morning, she woke very early. The king had already departed, leaving her alone in the tent. She got to her feet and paced in a wide circle. Her heart was not frozen now; it thudded hugely, pumping angry blood up through her hot face and into her shaking limbs. She was queen of nothing, then, or nothing more than a tumble of rocks on a cold hill, among people who thought her peculiar and trivial. There would be no proving anything to Oberon, no chance to show that she was as good and lovely and dutiful as the other daughter, the better daughter. There would be no reception to show up his other favorites, to display her own worth, to show that she was a queen among equals.

There was nothing else left for her, only this.

He promised me, she thought. Her hands and feet had gone oddly numb. *He promised me that if I took vows to him, it would bring me no sorrow.*

He lied.

Taryn pushed open the tent flap and stared around the bailey. Her eyes caught on something shining, silver, standing on its head in the grass next to the entrance of the neighboring tent: a short hand-axe. Perhaps one of the goblins who slept there had meant to split wood for their brazier this morning.

She walked forward and picked up the axe.

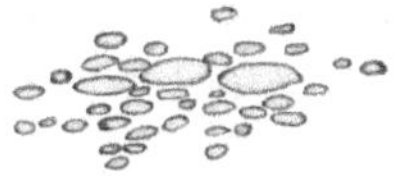

"You've been a great help," Ash said sleepily from the other side of the loft. "You've a fine eye for foraging. I wouldn't have found half so many kettle mushrooms if you hadn't been with me."

Taryn stared into the profound darkness over her head, where Ash had nailed long flat shingles and then hung a waxed length of wool to catch insects and crumbles of dirt falling from the underside of the earthen roof. Her back ached from stooping to pick the mushrooms, and her shoulders from the heavy baskets they'd used to carry them back to the witch's house.

She'd been in Ash's wood for eight days and slept in Ash's house for eight nights. She'd helped milk goats and cows, pour the milk into crocks to curdle, ladle curds into molds, churn butter from the whey; followed the witch out into the woods to harvest greens and mushrooms and wild strawberries; taken frames from the four massive wicker hives they kept on a high knoll and scraped the wax from them for candles and let the honey drip into pots; carried a bag of wheat to a narrow, fast, deep bit of a nearby stream where a little wheel stood to grind the flour for their seemingly endless supply of toast.

Every time Taryn flagged noticeably, the witch found a reason they needed to stop and take a rest, as well as a convenient stone or log where she could sit. She half-suspected that these waypoints did not actually exist until Ash asked for them, and the forest, obliging to its faithful tenant, pulled them close.

She did not want to stay in the shadowy house when the witch went out to work. The black boulder in her mind was diminishing in size, wobbling and growing less steady, and she knew that once it had rolled back she would have to leave the forest to do whatever it was she was not remembering now. She would rather stand close to Ash and listen to another story about how one of the Prince's cousins had had his sword and trews stolen by a vengeful clan of badgers.

Today when they had arrived back at the house after mushroom-hunting, Ash had taken her basket and whisked it away inside. "Just a minute," they called. "I've got something for you— just a minute—"

When Taryn finally poked her head around the door, a massive iron kettle sat on the hearth, and steam poured from its spout. Beneath it a little fire elemental danced and whistled, its many limbs flickering in and out of sight.

A wooden tub had appeared in the center of the room. It was large enough for Taryn to sit in, if she drew her knees up to her chest, and already filled with gently steaming water.

Ash appeared out of the shadowy recess under the loft, clutching some old quilts and a massive cake of soap. "Here we are," they said cheerfully. "Hiss-spit came right when I called, so it took hardly a minute—I've got some things for you to dry yourself with, and you can split off a piece of this—"

"Oh—I suppose I smell," Taryn said, staring longingly at the water.

"Not a bit of it," Ash said. "Or at least not more than any

of the other creatures roundabouts. Only—" Here they shifted the towels and soap to one arm, using the other to delicately pick up Taryn's hand and turn it over, so that the blistered palm faced upward. "—you've the skin of someone who perhaps doesn't do all her washing in cold water in a tin dish. As you've been such a hardy guest, I ought to do my best to be a fair host."

Ash busied themselves at the hearth, breaking up twigs for Hiss-spit the elemental, while Taryn stripped and submerged herself. The tub was a larger on the inside than the outside, so the water came up to her chin. She sat and and soaked and watched Ash move back and forth, sweeping up ashes and tidying the crockery. After a few minutes, the witch knelt and spoke to the fire elemental; it chirped at them and upended its kettle into a newly-appeared dish. The witch stripped off their grubby wool jacket and linen undershirt, turning a broad back to Taryn as they scrubbed their face and forearms.

There was a curious round mark, just above Ash's right shoulder blade, that looked like a many-pointed star. Taryn squinted at it. "What's that. . . freckle . . . on your back?"

Ash reached back to touch it, involuntarily. "It's a changeling mark," they said.

Taryn knew this should have meant something to her, but it didn't. She wanted to trace the mark with her fingers and kiss it. "So you are a changeling?"

"I am not," Ash said. "It's a long and unpleasant story." They finished washing and pulled the linen shift back over their head, hiding the star.

This was not how Taryn had wanted the conversation to go. She sat up a little straighter, so the water only just covered her breasts, and said to the broad back, "I need help washing my hair." They went still, a rag still pressed against the side of a crock they had started dusting. "It's very heavy."

"Right," the witch said. After a long pause, they set down the rag and walked back around the tub. Their hands were brisk and gentle as they unpinned the heavy black coils of hair from Taryn's head. They broke off a shard of the soap, held it under the hot water until it grew soft, and rubbed it firmly along her scalp.

They are washing me like I'm a goat who's been into something mucky, Taryn thought, part indignant and part drowsy with the soothing motion of the witch's hands over her head.

She wondered now, curled into a little bubble of warmth under the blankets, how long Ash had let her sleep in the tub before she had awakened enough to climb out and wrap herself in quilts. She wasn't tired anymore, though she had no particular inclination to leave the safe darkness of the loft.

"Ash," she whispered.

"Mm?"

"Have you had many other visitors here?"

There was a long, strange silence. "I have," they said. "You'll have seen most of them along the fence."

That was not the answer Taryn had expected. "You killed those people?" she demanded, thinking of their square, scarred, patient hands disentangling a bleating kid from a bramble.

"Oh, yes."

Taryn inched closer to the sound of their voice. "How do I know you won't put bits of me up on your fence?"

"Well, unless you've plans you haven't spoken about to murder me, rob me, or impress me into some army or another," came the very dry answer, "I'd rather not."

"No," Taryn said. "I didn't think so."

She'd eased across under the blanket until she could feel the heat of Ash's body up the side of her own. They slept flat on their back, one knee crooked, both arms flung over their head. She wriggled the rest of the way out of the shirt she'd borrowed to sleep in, reached forward, and laid a hand on the witch's belly.

"Hm?"

She pressed a little closer, and after a bit of nuzzling she was able to locate the soft spot at the base of their throat and kiss it.

"Oh," Ash sighed, their voice filled with understanding and sadness. "Dear one, I appreciate the thought, but it would be a disappointment for you."

"How?" Taryn asked mulishly, her fingers brushing their ribcage. "You're very good with your hands."

"That may be so, but I've got next to no experience in that

line. I wouldn't know—I wouldn't know how to make you happy."

"I can show you," she said, kissing a bit lower.

They caught their breath when she brushed the top of one breast with her cheek. She stopped, suddenly worried. "Should I—should I not touch you there?"

"It's all right," the witch said. "I keep them bound down because they're a nuisance and because people tended to get the wrong idea—when I went among people—but I haven't got anything against them, so to speak—"

Taryn breathed a little laugh and stretched her face up to push her nose into their ear. She took their earlobe between her teeth and sucked on it.

"Ah. That's—"

"You don't have to talk *all* the time," she whispered, wrapping her arm over them and dragging her nails lightly over their ribs.

"You—" Ash started to say, and Taryn bit their lower lip. She held it for a long minute, before letting go and pressing another kiss to the side of their mouth.

All she could hear for a moment was the witch's shallow breathing. Then, hoarsely, "Show me what to do."

Taryn fell back against the blankets, tugging gently until they rolled on top of her with a soft exhalation. For as short as the witch was, they were much heavier than she expected. She gasped a little at the weight, but wrapped her legs around their hips before they could pull away. Reaching upward, she stroked her hands over the back of their close-shorn head and then down again. Ash exhaled hugely. They lifted their upper body off her for a moment, bracing a hand on either side of her ribcage, and she could feel their eyes looking down on her. Could witches see in the dark? she wondered. She hoped they could. She braceleted their wrist with her fingers and lifted their hand, placing it on her breast.

Ash felt one breast and then the other with a firm, steady hand. Taryn heard them take a deep breath, and she guided their hand, pressing the thumb and forefinger around one nipple. Ash's touch was light. She put more pressure on their fingers. Taking the hint, they pinched, rolling the bud back and forth. She shuddered, deeply, pleasurably, before they dipped their head to the other breast and drew it into their mouth.

They stayed there for a long minute, squeezing one breast in their hand and one with their teeth. Taryn laughed and gasped a little, and felt Ash's head come up, felt the worried question form—

"No," she whispered. "Keep doing that. I like—I like when it hurts a little."

"Ah." Ash's voice sounded a little wry, but they went back down, this time biting the other breast and pinching the other. Finally they gave her breasts a firm rub all over, as if to check that the previous treatment had done them no harm. "Do you want—" Their hand moved down, over her belly.

"Yes. Yes, please."

Ash slid down her body and took a firm hold of her waist, nuzzling and then biting the soft skin above her navel.

"You're a sweet creature," they murmured.

Taryn caught her breath when they laced their hand through the curly hair between her legs and pulled lightly. But just as quickly they were smoothing it back, their fingers tracing around the most sensitive bit and parting the folds, so that they could put their mouth—

They were tentative at first, exploring with tongue and teeth, until her little moans made it clear they were going about things in the right way. They started to stroke her with their tongue, over the sensitive nub, again and again. One hand came up to rest on her inner thigh; they pressed two knuckles of the other just inside her.

Taryn let out a little cry. Ash briefly, lightly pressed their teeth into her, before suddenly pulling the nub into their mouth and sucking hard. She would have cried out again, but she couldn't breathe. It felt like her whole body had become one nerve that could only feel what Ash was doing. Every part of her clenched, then unclenched, and she gasped for breath.

"More?" That was gentle, a little hesitant, and she couldn't speak but she cupped the back of their head, trying to show them what she wanted. Their tongue returned to her, and they did the same thing again, this time rubbing her thigh firmly and sucking a little harder and longer.

When Taryn came back to herself, she was panting, lying on her side, and Ash had scooted up behind her back, one large arm wrapped firmly around her midsection, their face against her shoulder.

"I should—you haven't—let me—" Taryn tried to roll over, but she was so spent she could barely move.

"I've had enough excitement for the night, dear one," Ash said. They sounded as though they were already mostly asleep. "Have patience with me, for the goats certainly will not, come tomorrow morning."

PART TWO

The morning Taryn had eaten Ash's toast for nineteen days and slept in their loft for nineteen nights, she saw a wolf in the woods.

A path wound around the back of the oak that spread over the house, traced its way past the meadow where the cow and goats browsed, and finally dipped down to cross a clear, fast stream. Beside this spot spread a flat, smooth rock where she could kneel to do her washing—the vest and shirt and trousers she had been wearing when she arrived, and two large tunics that Ash procured from the depths of a crock.

Taryn wasn't sure if this stream was the same stream that turned the mill that ground the grain, and the witch looked shifty and vague when she asked. The path did not follow the same route from day to day. Or perhaps it was the trees that changed. The sunlit wood had strange shadows, brown and red pools that crept through the leaves when she turned her face away.

Her hands full with a clothing-basket, Taryn was not paying attention to the path or the shadows. She was thinking unsettled, warm thoughts about Ash, about how she had sat astride them while they lay in the grass that grew over the house's roof the afternoon before—how she had leaned forward suddenly and tickled them furiously under the ribs, and how Ash had shouted with laughter. Underneath this snaked another image, another face smiling up at her, a different set of hands holding her waist as she straddled their—his?—hips.

A bit of rotten wood cracked under her foot, and she looked up, frowning. The gnarled pine scooping its branches low over the path did not look familiar. She stepped forward, uncertain, twisting to look behind herself.

When she turned back a wolf stood in the path, blocking it from edge to edge, its lips lifted over its teeth in a silent snarl.

Taryn froze, staring into the wolf's eyes. They were all shades of brown, clay and walnut and amber, shifting from one into another. Its ruff stood up stiffly all around its face. She had never seen a wolf in the flesh before, but this one's legs seemed too long, its fangs too curved, its ears too pointed.

The moment broke, and she hurled the basket of laundry at the beast. It leaped to one side, off the path, and vanished among the trees.

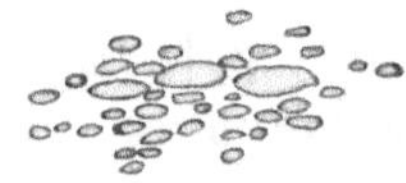

Ash was not surprised when Taryn told them about the wolf.

"He hangs around here sometimes," they said, scooping a ladle of curd out of a massive crock and dumping it into the first of a series of clay jars with holes punched through the base. "If I can spare it, I take a bucket of whey out past the stream for him when I know he's about."

"Won't that draw other wild animals?" Taryn asked.

"This is a magical wood," Ash said, amused. "If he's here at all, he's already got his own troubles."

She was quiet for a minute, wondering what sort of troubles a wolf might have. "How many times have you seen him?"

"Oh, dozens. Here, put these on the rack," the witch went on, passing her some filled molds. "I was alone here for a year or two, and then after that I started to see him flitting about behind the trees every few months."

"Alone?" Taryn repeated. She thought of the fence, with its bone-shards, and then of Ash's stories, in which a nameless friend always held the sword or brought the horse or found the last ingredient for a charm. "Did no one from—from your old life come to visit you here? The person—the people you went adventuring with."

"They'd have a hard time finding me," Ash said, staring down into the crock of whey, a sharp divot between their eyebrows. "I suppose that was how I wanted it, at the time."

"Would you want to see them again, now?"

"Oh, maybe." Ash looked up at the ceiling for a minute, as though an answer might be written on the beams. "There's a few of them I'd pour out an ale for." They heaved a huge sigh and hoisted the crock of whey to their shoulder, before disappearing out the door of the cottage. A few minutes later they ducked back in, their hands empty. Taryn wondered where they'd put it. It usually took them nearly an hour to take the whey out to the part of the forest where the semi-feral pigs that Ash turned into bacon roamed.

"I think you should go looking for them," she said suddenly. The boulder in her mind had gotten very small in the last two days, and in fact was more of a dark pebble that she kept her thoughts trained on so she would not have to consider the troublesome things spilling out on all sides of it. She knew with painful certainty that she must leave soon, and the image of Ash making cheese alone in the house made her throat close up.

They rubbed their hands together as they walked toward the hearth, not quite looking at her, and Taryn wondered if she'd crossed some sort of invisible line. The silence felt solid in the blueing light of the evening.

"The trouble is," the witch said, so softly she could barely hear over the low crackle of the cooking fire, "I came away where no one could find me because I wasn't sure anyone would be looking. And I'm still not sure."

Taryn unfolded herself from the top of the chair where she'd been perched and slipped up beside them, wrapping her arms around their barrel chest and stretching a bit to put her chin on top of their bristly head. "You said they were your great friends," she said. "With you through years of—of blood and nonsense."

Ash was stiff for a moment, and Taryn's gut jerked in fear of being pushed away. Another moment passed, and they slumped and reached up to cradle her elbow. "Blood and nonsense is right," they muttered. "And it was full of that. But at the last—well. At the last, who knows what they might think of me, fool that I proved myself."

"You're not a fool," Taryn whispered.

"I have been," Ash said, turning fully into her arms and carefully wrapping both of their own about her waist. "But whether I still am ought not bother you. So."

"So," Taryn repeated. She let herself be pulled down onto the warm stones in front of the hearth.

When she woke, the house was dark and cold. A few coals still glowed at the back of the fireplace. A heavy blanket had been draped over her and tucked in under her feet, and a pillow put under her head. Ash had gone from her side, but when she stretched out her hand the space beside her was still faintly warm.

The embers cast the faintest of lights into the room. It had been cloudy all day, and no light from the moon or stars shone through the small windows. A whisper of a cold breeze touched her face. If she squinted, a line of darker shadow traced the edge of the door. Someone had opened it. Taryn thought she saw another shadow—a long, low shadow—moving across the room. Was that Ash? It wasn't the right shape. Were they crouched down? Fear jerked at her stomach, and she felt as though she could barely breathe, let alone move or cry out. Where was Ash?

A coal sparked, and the light glanced across a pair of amber eyes.

"So you've decided to come inside." That was Ash's voice, but pitched so low she could barely hear it. "I wondered if you might."

The shadow-wolf stopped in the center of the room. Its head swung toward the fireplace, and Taryn hastily closed her eyes, as though it were some sort of nightmare that she could wish away —

"No, let her sleep. She's no trouble to you. Come here and let me have a look at you."

Taryn opened her eyes the tiniest sliver. A flint clicked against a piece of steel in the dark, before a flame sparked up. Ash, seated at the table, touched the lit wick to a candle and held it out toward the wolf. The flickering light made it look even more huge.

A scream built in Taryn's throat as it padded closer to Ash, but the witch slumped in their chair, watching the beast thoughtfully but tiredly.

As soon as the wolf stepped within arms'-length, they reached out and took firm hold of its face. Taryn choked. Her heart sped up. "Well, you're transformed, that's obvious enough," they murmured. "You've been a fine enough neighbor to me, these past ten years. Would you have help to change back?"

The wolf momentarily rested its great head in the crook of Ash's arm. "Very well, then."

They picked up something from the table that Taryn could not see and fiddled with it, as though untying a knot and then retying a different one. Strange words twisted and unfolded in the silence, just below the range of her hearing, spoken by many creatures deep underground.

The wolf's skin writhed and smoothed itself as the words did, untying itself from around the body inside and then retying itself in a new shape. The wolf stood up. Taryn could not see his face, but she knew the tall shoulders and pointed ears. Suddenly her fear was replaced entirely by anger.

Ash's face, half visible to her around the shadow of the standing figure, crumpled just a little. "It's you, then."

"It's me," said the goblin king, his voice equally low.

The witch was silent, staring at nothing, apparently collecting their thoughts. "I didn't—" They stopped, opened, closed their mouth. "It's been a while, I suppose." Taryn didn't think that was what they had meant to say.

"Just short of twelve years," he said, his voice very dry.

"And you've known where I was, all this time."

"No. It took me a year and a half to find you."

"But after that—"

"I didn't think you wanted to be found."

"Maybe not," said Ash. "But why now? I haven't got anything to give you. I'm busy enough with the cows and the goats, and busier yet now. That girl there—the young woman—she's been here nearly three weeks, and she needs looking after—doesn't have a memory to her name, doesn't know where she was going before she fell into the wood—"

"I expect she'll remember quickly enough when she sees me," the king said. Now there was an edge to his voice. "She's mine. I brought her here because I thought — I thought you might be able to do something with her."

Ash repeated, as though dazed, "Yours? Your—your—"

"My wife."

"Then she's Oberon's daughter," they said, in a hiss of breath.

Taryn did not even have a moment to react to the way Ash's voice contorted with pain and anger when it spoke that name—her *father's* name—before the king interrupted.

"No."

"But—"

"She's not."

What does he mean, I'm not? Taryn thought, her heart pounding.

"Then you've broken your vow."

"No," he said. "I kept it to the letter."

"*Ah.*" There was a wealth of meaning in that sound, but Taryn could not interpret it. "I see. Where is—the other daughter?"

The other daughter. *The better daughter.* Her stomach twisted. She had never been allowed to ask questions about where that other, more-loved child had gone.

"In the country where Taryn was born," the king said.

"No. *No.*" Ash's voice was furious, barely controlled. "It *will not stand.*"

"It does not have to," he said, his words careful. "A changeling cannot stay in the same house with the child it has replaced."

Ash made a sound like a sob. Taryn's mind whirled. *A changeling?*

"No," they said finally. "No, of course not."

Taryn woke in the loft under a vast array of blankets. The night before felt like a terrible dream, shadowy nonsense layered on nonsense—she couldn't be a *changeling*—she was a king's daughter—she was a king's wife—she was a queen—she lived in a palace—she lived in a tent in a castle—

—she was a witch's helper who lived in the forest and milked goats—

—who *was* she?

She rolled over onto her elbows and crept toward the edge of the loft to peer out.

The goblin king sat at the table, eating toast.

Ash had cleared away the bits of riffraff from the center of the floor and was in the process of drawing a large, complicated shape in ashes on the flagstones. As she watched, they clambered to their feet, then walked slowly around the image, muttering unintelligibly, before changing direction and walking the other way, this time dropping a small object—feather, acorn, bone, feather again — in each repeated point of the pattern.

They stopped and clapped, and the shape came off the floor with a crack and folded itself immediately into a tiny, glimmering ball, which Ash plucked out of the air and handed to the king. He took it and put it in his pocket.

"That ought to make you less noticeable, anyway," they said. "Wizard in a port town showed me that one."

There didn't seem to be any point to pretending she was still asleep. Taryn rearranged her tunic under the covers and crawled across to the ladder. Once her feet touched the floor, she pointedly didn't look up until she'd smoothed down her braids and pinned them back on top of her head.

The king was watching her with an unreadable expression. He wasn't eating now.

"Good morning," Ash said, turning. "How much did you hear last night?"

Taryn deflated a bit. "I—some."

"Sit down, and I'll get you something hot to drink. There's another half-loaf of bread to be toasted. Then you know we leave today to fetch Oberon's daughter back from where she's pretending to be you."

"No," she said, in a very small voice.

"Well, now you do." Ash turned away from her, kneeling to slice bread on the hearth and slot the pieces into a rack over the coals. They stood, dusting their hands on their grimy wool jacket. "You don't have to come, if you'd rather not," they said quietly, without looking back at her. "The wood will hold you safe until we return. And then—well. Then you'll have choices to make about where you go, but those will keep."

Taryn wished she were back in the loft or in the meadow with the animals or anywhere, really, that wasn't here. "But not back to my—not back to Oberon's palace," she said, her voice embarrassingly thin. "That's not one of the choices."

"You lost that option when you followed me freely from his court," the goblin king said. *As you should have known,* he did not say but clearly meant.

"You didn't tell me," Taryn said, angry and helpless and frightened. "You didn't tell me I wouldn't be able to go back. I didn't know—"

He shrugged, his face dispassionate. "Better be taken from under the hill now, when only eleven years have passed, than wait for the—*other daughter*—to grow tired of your birthright, and be cast out into the human world in a hundred years as an old, old woman."

Taryn drew in a deep breath. She would not weep. She could not weep.

"Stop," the witch said quietly. "There's no use talking about it now."

She turned toward Ash, her eyes cloudy with unshed tears, and saw that they had produced a small knapsack and a number of useful items: a bronze knife, a flask, two flints, a length of rope, several small packages.

"Do you have horses waiting for us on the other side?" they asked the king.

"I do. Lilith and Nel. She can't ride," he added, jerking his chin at Taryn.

"She can take turns with both of us, then."

"Nel won't carry her."

"Have you *asked* Nel if he will carry her?" they inquired, eyebrows high.

"I haven't said that I'll go," Taryn interjected.

Unperturbed, Ash nodded. "Very well. I must go up to the meadow to make arrangements with the oaks to look after my beasts. Think on it. We'll leave when I return."

They stuffed the assemblage of useful items in the small knapsack, leaned it against the doorframe, and slipped outside.

Taryn clenched her fists. The mug Ash had set out for her, across the table from the king, still steamed gently. Beside it they had made a pile of toast and cheese on a plate. She could not quite imagine herself walking across the room to sit in that chair and eat while facing him. Instead she stared intensely at his long-fingered, clawed hand resting on the table, her jaw locked.

The hand turned over on the table, and the fingers curved into a beckoning.

"Come here."

"Why should I?"

"Because you are my wife, and I told you to."

"I didn't agree to that," she hissed, looking him in the eye.

"You don't know what you agreed to," he said, and her stomach churned.

"I know that you are very casual with your vows. Neither harm nor sorrow," she shot back.

"Come here," he repeated. "Ash will be at least an hour, talking to the trees."

Taryn went, and she refused to think more about it than to acknowledge the same pull deep in her belly that led her away from Oberon's throne and through a door into another world. What this king wanted of her in this moment in this little dark house was clear enough, even if whether he had followed her into the wood to get it —or why—was not.

He lifted his beckoning hand to her, and she took it, noting rather sardonically that he did not seem inclined to shed his claws for her benefit this time.

His eyes moved over her face and down her neck. The tunic, one of Ash's, had slipped down over one shoulder. The baggy garment fell to her mid-thighs, but she had not had a moment to sort through their stash of clothing to find trews or leggings, leaving her legs bare.

"Take it up," he said quietly, his other hand flicking the hem of the tunic. "I want to look at you."

Taryn stared back, her mind a wordless tumult of anger and hunger. The barest hint of puzzlement threaded its way through: *why?* Surely after what she'd done to the shrine of his mother's people the king wanted nothing to do with her, unless it was to pay her back in some way.

Had he meant to pay her back by leaving her with Ash?

She smoothed one palm up her thigh, hiking the tunic up onto her hip. The night before last she had lain in the loft, her head resting on Ash's chest, her back against their front, and they had stroked the front of her thigh just so. Her hand slid higher, to rest in the crease of her hip. The king's eyes flicked from her hand to her face and then back to her hand. He licked his lips.

Taryn lifted the tunic higher, uncovering the juncture of her legs. A cool breeze from beneath the door whispered against her. Ash had touched just there, pressing up and inside, Taryn's fingers guiding theirs. She dragged her hand up her body to her ribcage, letting the fabric drape around her navel.

"Ash hasn't let you starve, then," the king said. Taryn, startled, would have jerked away, but the hand holding hers tightened, and the claws of his free hand caressed the slight curve of her belly.

Taryn hesitated, unsure, as he continued to draw light circles over her stomach. It felt very good, and she couldn't read the expression in his tawny eyes. If she hadn't known better, she would have thought it was something like pleasure. "No," she finally relented. The hand holding hers slid to her wrist, and the pad of his thumb massaged her palm.

The king reached across the table to the plate that Ash had left for her and broke off a piece of toast. He held it to her lips. When she didn't immediately open them, he pressed the bit of food there, smearing butter and jam onto her cheek and chin.

She parted her teeth, and he pushed his fingers into her mouth. Taryn bit him—lightly—and considered biting him in seriousness, but the food tasted so good. She was suddenly terribly aware of how hungry she was and clutched the tunic against her body. When the king took another piece, she let him feed it to her and sucked the extra bits of jam off his fingers. His hand lingered on her mouth, the sharp claw of the thumb tracing her lip.

He fed her a bit more before letting his hand ghost downward again. She'd let the tunic drop, but he pushed it back up, baring her breasts. He stroked these as well, as though he had missed seeing them, missed seeing her—

Don't think it, Taryn told herself. It will only hurt.

The king tucked the hem of the tunic through the neck of the garment, leaving her body exposed to his eyes. He dragged his fingers down her midline, almost absently stopping where her thighs pressed together. His hand stopped there, and he waited, his eyes sharp on her face.

Taryn lifted one heel from the ground, crooking her knee. He slid his hand around the back of her thigh, and she let him lift that leg until her foot rested on the wood of the chair between his legs. The cool breeze from the door was even colder now, and she shivered as he spread her folds apart. She shivered again as he rubbed there with his palm, though now she was growing warm all over, in spite of her nakedness—

A ceramic bottle sat at the center of the table, a heavy round thing covered in smooth blue glaze. Sometimes Ash put flowers in it, when they remembered, though they had not remembered for the past week. The king picked it up now, his eyes speculative. Taryn considered it too, as much as she could consider when her whole body beat with increasing hunger. He leaned forward, finally letting go of her wrist to wrap one arm around her waist. She couldn't see what he did with his other hand, but she felt him push the bottle inside her. It was like and unlike being underneath the king; he was larger but not so hard. It was cold and smooth and slid through her like—like—

She came with a choked noise and almost fell over; the arm around her waist tightened. He drew the bottle out, and she shuddered hugely. A moment later the sound of ceramic shattering touched her ears. Dizzy, Taryn let her head drop, and the king guided it onto his shoulder.

"You will come with us," he said against her ear. "To cast Oberon's daughter out."

"Yes," she said bitterly.

If I am not Oberon's daughter, she thought, then who am I?

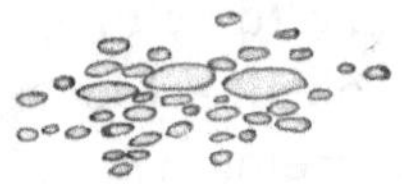

Nel was a tall chestnut gelding whose ears went back immediately upon smelling Taryn. He whickered and danced sideways toward Lilith, who huffed air irritably and resumed eating pine needles.

The goblin king had not tied either horse up in the dark, cold forest on the other side of the world-door that crossed into Ash's enchanted wood. After the three of them walked through— the horizon swung briefly around Taryn as one set of trees exchanged themselves for another—he whistled, a long, low, wavering sound that snaked away through the wet trunks. They stood in awkward silence for one minute—five—fifteen minutes, before two equine forms resolved themselves from the shadows. One of them was black, six-legged, and fiery-eyed, and the other was Nel.

Ash, unphased by the horse's anxiety, approached him with a

toasted cheese sandwich held loosely in one hand, a knapsack hanging from their shoulders.

"Hallo, gentlebeast," they said. The horse's nose followed the scent of the sandwich. His ears flicked forward again, as though he recognized Ash. The witch broke off a little piece and offered it on the flat of their palm. He snuffled it up and butted their shoulder gently.

Ash reached up and scratched under the horse's jaw. They stood together for a long minute like that. Taryn watched, a slow, strange longing pressing down on her heart. She had barely been able to look at the king since they had left the house under the oak tree. Ash had been polite but quiet, as though they had only just met —as though they hadn't really met at all.

She hadn't meant to choose—she hadn't *wanted* to choose—

Nel's nostrils flared, and he poked Ash's sandwich-holding hand inquisitively.

"This is Taryn," Ash said, nodding in her direction. She nervously stepped forward, and Ash, not quite smiling, tipped their head to one side. She held out her hand, and Ash laid the rest of the sandwich in it. "She's a friend. Be still now," they said, this last to her. "He'll come around."

The king watched this exchange with eyebrows high. Along with his claws, his tusks had come back, and he looked very fierce indeed. Taryn wondered uneasily whether a goblin might ride through the human kingdoms in full daylight, or if they would need to make their way by the moon. At least the king, unlike many of his cousins, did not have a long, tufted tail.

While she was considering this, Ash crawled up onto Nel's saddle, which was long enough for two people to sit, if they crowded together.

"Here, help her up," they said to the king.

"It would be easier if she rode with me."

"It'll be easier for Nel while he's still fresh. Once he's tired, the fairy itch will get to him faster."

"The itch won't get to Lilith at all."

"I want to ride with Ash," Taryn broke in sharply.

"I think Nel's resigned himself to the situation," the witch said placatingly, "so long as there's food along the way."

Before Taryn could fully catch her breath, the king had seized her around the waist and tossed her up onto the horse's back. She cried out and thudded heavily into Ash, who twisted around to take hold of her.

"*Steady,*" they hissed at Nel, who was clearly thinking of rearing. The king strode to his nose and gripped the halter. He whinnied and then subsided, but his flanks quivered. "No thanks for that," Ash said crossly.

He shrugged. Lilith snorted hugely and snapped off a great branch with a jerk of her head, which seemed to be her version of a shrug.

Ash twisted to face the back of Nel's head again and gestured for Taryn to reach into the knapsack. "There's something for you at the top," they muttered. "Keep it close, but don't draw it just yet."

Her fingers closed around a long, narrow scabbard inside the bag. She drew it out and shoved it through her belt, her fingers quickly tracing the shape of the hilt. It was a long-knife of the sort the goblins used for hunting, only the blade was made of bronze.

Ash was not a particularly good rider, Taryn realized as they set out, picking their way behind the king and his great mare into the ever-denser and ever-darker forest. They took every bump and root as a jolt to the tailbone. The only thing that kept them from falling off was that Nel was terribly concerned that this should not happen, and by extension and grudgingly, that Taryn should not fall either. She clutched at the horse's back with her legs and tried not to clutch equally tightly to the witch in front of her. They went at a slow, careful walk, pausing every hour or two for Ash to produce more treats for Nel from the knapsack. Taryn suspected the bag had significantly larger interior capacity than exterior dimensions.

The king astride Lilith rode in far-ranging circles around them, disappearing for long stretches of time only to appear soundlessly just behind Nel. He did not comment on their slow progress.

"Are we going back to the goblins?" Taryn whispered, during one of these absences. It seemed very important not to make too much noise under these black trees.

"No," said Ash, their voice no louder than hers. "That road into the human kingdom has been closed for a long time, and it would be very noticeable if I were to open it now. I don't suppose we would get very far if we were recognized for who we are. She— the one who we seek knows that the king is no friend of hers. We are taking another way, one we passed by a long time ago."

Taryn wanted to ask which story the road had been in, but she bit her lip.

The forest grew so dark that when she stretched her hand out before her, her eyes burned with an absence where they expected her pale fingers to be. Far away in the trees, lich-fires winked in and out.

Suddenly the king was there, the fire of Lilith's eyes illuminating the smallest ring around him.

"Give her over," he said, leaning across. "You cannot work if you are spending yourself keeping Nel quiet and her in her seat."

"Fair enough," Ash said, and their voice sounded so strained that Taryn wondered what magic they had been already doing in the dark, visible to no eyes but their own hands.

The king pulled her off Nel's saddle and settled her in front of himself, but he paused for a moment. Taryn felt his arm moved behind her, as though he clasped Ash's shoulder. "Steady?"

"Steady enough," they said. "Here—" They passed something across the gap between the horses, which the king accepted, but then pressed silently against Taryn's stomach. She took it, silent too. It was a little wooden disc, carved in a smooth whorl across the top, a leather cord knotted through it. She pulled it over her neck. Every inch of her skin tingled and fizzed for a moment as the charm settled over her.

"There," Ash said suddenly. "Now we're for it."

Taryn jerked her head around. Several of the lich-lights had grown much brighter and larger in the last minute. Something whistled by her face, and she felt the goblin king snarl and lurch to one side.

It was too dark to see exactly what was attacking them or from where. Taryn tried to speak a light charm, but the word met the uncertain void about them with a sucking noise and then an absence. The lich-lights were not entirely solid nor entirely magical. One of them, drawn by the spell, wrapped itself around her and insinuated cold tendrils of despair around her mind before the charm at her throat flashed with heat. The lich-light screamed, a sound simultaneously inside her and echoing from very far away, and shattered with a foul, acidic smell.

Another light sliced through the darkness at them, only to be seized and hurled away. The liches had partially dissolved the reality around them, and the trees had become transparent, sooty smears against the black. The king drew both legs underneath himself and rose into a crouch on Lilith's back. He was almost entirely goblin now, and Taryn could feel his long-fingered feet digging into the leather of the saddle behind her. In response Lilith planted all six of her hooves and lunged about herself like a striking snake. One of the lich-lights succeeded in scaring Nel into a short gallop, but she could not see in what direction or how far he had carried Ash.

Taryn drew the long-knife from its scabbard; it gleamed with a vicious glow. One of the lich-lights darted at her, and she struck. It squealed and wheeled away, its light dimming.

Goblins smelled almost exactly like Ash's goats, she thought nonsensically, as she searched the darkness for lich-lights and tensed for the next blow. Six of them had formed a cluster ahead and to the left of Lilith. Their glow was a terrible one that did not make it any easier to make out what was happening, but after a minute Taryn understood that the lights were trying to unseat the witch, to pull them down into the darkness. Nel screamed, a horrible sound that the lich-lights swallowed up.

Taryn's mind whirled. She thought the king could see in the dark, but she certainly couldn't. She would have liked to throw the knife and strike at the biggest of the lich-lights, crouched in an attitude of a spider mantling over its stunned prey, but she might just as easily hit Ash.

Most of the magic she knew required something physical to ground it, time to speak a chant, space to draw figures on the ground. She could not, as Ash seemingly did, talk objects and plants and animals into accommodating her. Except—she thought of Oberon in his palace, when he'd just received word that one of his least favorite liege-ladies had arrived under the hill. He had wanted to offend, but only just so much. He had sent dozens of copies of himself walking through the halls of the palace, flimsy simulacra that would respond to a greeting with a ridiculous little wave and a jeering smile before disappearing around another corner—

She thought of Ash and Nel riding together, their warmth and smell and the shape their bodies made, and blew over her palm. Three, or possibly four, shapes unfolded themselves from her breath, merged outlines that made the witch and the horse into a single, lumpy beast, fleeing as though they feared for their shadowy lives. Taryn caught her breath—the king seized another lich-light and tore it in half—but two of the entities crowding around Ash flashed away, hunting her illusions.

Lilith careened forward, drawing even with the remaining enemies. The biggest lich-light had grown brighter as it came apart into bulbous, pulsing singularities.

"Hold," the king said. "I'm going to jump."

Taryn held her knife low against Lilith's side and leaned so far forward that she lay almost flat on the horse's back. The king launched himself into the constellation of sickly-beating lights that the growing lich had transformed into. The acidic smell came again, this time more rancid and stronger. The lich-light screamed with a noise like a thousand pieces of chalk all grating against each other. The charm flared against Taryn's neck, so hot this time that she could feel her flesh burning.

Lilith pressed her side tight against something in the darkness, and when Taryn groped downward she felt sweat-slick horse hide, shivering with fear and effort. She reached further, and her hands found a sticky, cold arm.

"Ash," she said, but the word was lost in another cacophony of lich screams. "*Ash!*"

"Here," came a wobbly response. "Oh, mercy upon us. Let me see the charm."

The cold arm which she had seized didn't move, but Ash's whole body rotated and they grabbed desperately with their other hand. Taryn found their fingers with her own and pressed them to the wooden whorl at her throat.

"Be shamed, O thou who art but dust," Ash whispered, "be shamed, and begone from here."

There was no sound, but a great vibration shook the air, the earth, and every one of Taryn's bones, as though a great forest of trees had simultaneously been felled all at once and come crashing to the ground. Everything went white, and then black again, before resolving itself into a sort of gray, smoking haze.

Suddenly there were no lich-lights, only cold, wet tree trunks and the twilight under their branches. The goblin king crouched before them on the ground, his clothes rent, his tusks and eyes gleaming, a crest of bristling hair running over his skull and down his back.

"Old friend," Ash said, barely louder than they had spoken the incantation. "You'll have to lead Nell. We don't have much time to leave this place."

The king sprung from his place on the ground, landing on Lilith's massive hindquarters like a great cat and spinning around to take hold of Taryn and Nel's reins. He made a peculiar clicking sound with his mouth, and both horses broke into a canter.

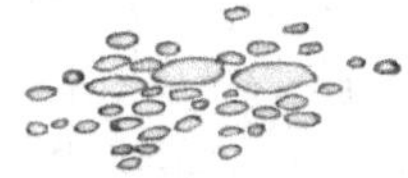

Nel had been badly slashed along his forequarters and was so shaken that Lilith would not stand more than a few paces off from him. Her fangs made her rather poor at grooming, so she nuzzled him impatiently. Taryn rummaged in Ash's knapsack and came up with a small armful of golden hay, which she layered on top of a stump for Nel.

They had emerged from the black wood onto a dusty, rutted road, the late afternoon sun throwing long shadows across the ground. The goblin king stopped the horses almost immediately, leading them into a copse of scrubby trees to make camp. He produced a single-edged blade half again as long as Taryn's knife and cleared an area wide enough to dig a fire pit.

Ash slid or fell off of Nel and crouched at the base of a tree, holding their immobile right arm tight to their body with their left hand. They had turned away when Taryn had first approached them, mumbling, " 'm all right—just give me a minute—get my bearings—" She had moved away uneasily. They'd need water no matter what, she told herself, and, after collecting two large flasks from Lilith's saddlebags, plunged into the trees toward the sounds of a stream running over rocks.

The stream was narrow and the water dirty. It took Taryn much longer than she intended to fill both flasks. When she reemerged into the camp with one under each arm, Ash now sat by the tree, head dropped to their chest, unmoving. The king stood over them, looking more bewildered than she had ever seen him look.

Taryn swore at him, dropping the flasks in the leaf litter and falling to her knees by the witch. She reached out and delicately probed along their right arm. Her stomach flipped over when she found the first break, but it dropped somewhere deep into the earth when she found the second.

Ash retched a little with the pain of having her touch their arm. "Don't," they said. "It's fine."

"It isn't fine," Taryn said, aware that she was crying. "How do I fix this?" she said to the king, her voice well on its way to a scream. "What do I *do?*"

"Don't bother him," Ash muttered. "Always look after myself."

"I *will* bother him," Taryn said wildly. "I—"

"Fetch me as many long, straight sticks as you can," the king said in a strange voice. He knelt beside Taryn. His crest and tusks had disappeared. *"Go,"* he hissed, when he saw that she hadn't moved.

Taryn got to her feet, momentarily unsure if they would even hold her upright, and started toward the other side of the camp, where she'd seen a tall pine sapling. Ash let out a little cry, and she whirled; the king had lowered them onto their back. She turned away, as shaky as if her own body were full of broken bones. She cut a dozen straight pine boughs with the long-knife and hastily stripped them of their twigs and needles.

The next hour was indescribably horrible. Ash moved into and out of consciousness, sometimes weeping in half-awake pain as the king maneuvered their arm into a position that could be splinted. They were too exhausted to do any magic that might speed the process, and Taryn had never learned any healing enchantments. She knew the king was some sort of magician himself, but she wasn't sure if it was a sort that could be used to help Ash, or if he'd spent himself fighting the lich-lights. As it was, his long fingers moved over their arm with slow care, and his eyes flicked regularly to their face with an almost feverish intensity.

"It's done," he said, after a very long time layering and tying the sticks into a hard splint that would not allow either of the two broken places to move. Ash had finally passed out completely and lay white-faced upon the leaf litter, barely visible in the blueing twilight.

"What happened?" Taryn whispered. She had knelt across from him, on the other side of Ash's limp body.

"One of the—one of them must have thrown Ash down on a rock or something," the king said, wiping sweat from his brow. "They could have been unhorsed and climbed back on, and I— neither of us—would have been able to see."

"Will they—" she started to ask, but she couldn't form the words around the knot in her throat. "Will—will—"

"Stop." He reached out and pressed two knuckles against her mouth.

Taryn closed her eyes.

"I know it looks very bad," he said. "They've a few broken ribs, as well. But Ash is—I can't explain to you what Ash is. They'll be all right. We'll camp for two days and then carry on."

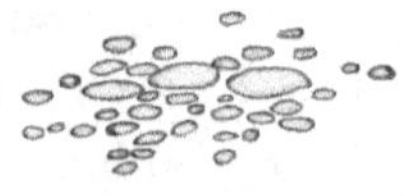

Ash lay unmoving in the leaf litter through the night. The

king lit a fire just before sunset, but Taryn, afraid what would happen if the witch became too cold, crept close to them and pressed against their unwounded side. They did not wake or respond to her, and their breathing was shallow and fast.

She did not think she could sleep with what felt like a fist gripping her heart, but she woke with a cold nose to moonlight streaming through the branches. The king had laid down beside her and wrapped his ragged clothes over both her and the witch. The horses snorted and shifted at the other side of the clearing.

The next time she woke from troubled dreams, the air was misty and gray. A rumbling snore filled the camp, which after a minute she localized to Nel.

Ash's breathing had slowed and deepened, but they did not stir when Taryn propped herself up to look carefully into their face, or when she tentatively brushed her lips over one cheekbone. She thought their face was a little ruddier, but they remained very, very still.

Mid-morning she felt the king's hand upon her elbow.

"Come away," he said. "They will recover no faster with your brooding, and there are things that must be done."

"Must?" snapped Taryn. "*Must?*"

"Must, unless you would eat dust and leaves. Lilith will look after Ash." The six-legged horse stomped her middle hooves and sidled closer to where Ash lay.

Taryn found herself numbly being boosted onto Nel's back. Someone—the king? Or could Ash work in their dreams?—had done some bit of magic, as the slash in his forequarters had half-scarred over during the night.

The king mounted behind her and turned the horse's nose toward the road.

It quickly became apparent that Ash had been maintaining some sort of charm all of the previous day to keep Nel calm while carrying a woman who reeked of fairy magic. Despite the king's much better seat, the horse nearly threw both of them three times in the first hour. Finally the king lifted Taryn down, dismounted, and walked Nel, who, freed from the panicked itching of the fairies, dipped his head in shame.

They walked in silence for a long time. Taryn worried over Ash in the leaves. She trusted Lilith, more or less, but if their condition took a sudden turn for the worse, what could a horse do? Could they get back to Ash in time? A small stream curved close to the road, and Nel stopped to drink.

She frowned at the horse. When she looked up, her eyes caught the king's. He had been staring at her intently.

"Ash will be all right," he said.

"How do you *know?* Anyone—any human with those injuries—"

"Witches become something else than human, and Ash has been a witch for a long time," he said shortly. "It would be better if you turned your mind toward finding Oberon's daughter."

"Do you know where she is?" Taryn asked. Her heart had eased slightly at his calm assertion of Ash's resilience, but it sped up again now.

"I think I do," the king said carefully. "The fairy changeling takes the place of the child they steal, and I know what place she would have wanted to take, and what human child Oberon would have deigned to have under his hill."

Taryn was silent, swimming through the gray haze in her head and finding nothing. "So you know who I—who I was. What is— what is my real family like, then?" Her voice felt like it was coming from very far away.

Nel lifted his head from the stream and stuck his wet nose into the king's ear. The goblin snorted and lifted a hand to scratch his jaw. "If she is where I think she is, there isn't much of the family left. The parents—the parents of that child died five years ago, in an accident. There was a younger sister."

"I don't remember any of that," Taryn said tightly. "I don't remember anyone."

"You might never remember any of it, or only pieces of it. Oberon's magic is very powerful."

Taryn swallowed. The king looked at her, the expression on his face almost unbearable in its tenderness. She turned away and walked ahead as quickly as possible.

The road cut through straggly trees before emerging onto a

hilltop, where it looked down over a patchwork of fields and farms.

Taryn stared into a shimmering wave of blue-green grass that rolled away from them, her stomach sinking.

It all felt terribly, painfully familiar. It *smelled* familiar. But she couldn't *remember.*

If she wasn't Oberon's daughter, then who was she? What had it felt like to be that other girl?

They rounded another hill and were confronted with a village, a smattering of stone houses strung along either side of the road as it descended into a valley. At the bottom of the town, the way split. In the junction sat a colonnaded building, a golden standard on a pole in front of it. Taryn stared at the glimmering shape atop the pole and felt a monstrous headache bloom behind her left eyebrow.

"What is that?" she asked, rubbing her face. Nel, curiously enough, seemed to be having the opposite reaction from her own; he had stopped, stretching his neck out and pointing his ears forward toward the structure, his tail swishing with interest.

"A temple to the highest god these humans worship," the goblin king said. "There is one in every town."

He dropped Nel's reins, and the horse took off at a trot toward the building and disappeared through the dark open doorway.

"What—" But the king was already striding down the village's single street toward a crooked, many-storeyed building jammed between two foursquare houses. A bronze statue of a dog with a single paw lifted and its nose in the air stood on the heavy lintel over the door. He lifted the latch and ducked inside.

Taryn followed him. The room they entered was paneled in dark wood. A massive hearth split the back, and casks lined both side walls. Two women, one in a tunic and heavy skirt and the other wearing a tunic and full pants tied up at the knee, were wrestling one of these casks up onto a table.

The second one addressed the king in a full, stern voice in a language Taryn did not know—

—except she *did* know it—

—*Keep your patience, we've not even put the pie in for tonight,* clicked into her brain thirty seconds after, when the king was already responding in the same tongue—

—but what language was it? When had she heard it? Who had spoken it to her?

Her chest felt very tight and her throat like it was closing. She backed away toward the door, and then turned and fled through it down the street.

Her headache made itself known again as soon as the golden standard came into sight. Angrily, she strode toward it. It had no right to make her feel this ill.

As she approached the pole it stood on, the shape at the top did not resolve itself. The light continued to glare off it painfully. Taryn went on towards the temple behind it. Up close, this building was hardly less ramshackle than the little public house where she'd left the king. The walls were built of uneven stones and rather a lot of mortar, and none of the pillars holding up the portico were quite straight. The great doorway stood open, without any hint of a door.

The interior was even more puzzling; the floor was strewn with straw and lit from above by several small holes punched in the roof. The rafters were bare. The central hall continued all the way down the building to another large, open doorway. It was, to all intents and purposes, a stone barn with a porch.

In the center of the temple, there were two niches in both opposing walls, each holding a lumpy white statue of a figure with the face worn away. Taryn walked past these and felt another unhappy jolt as she recognized the figures. They were the same—*being*—neither male nor female, but all things together and something entirely other than all of these things, and their name was

—

She hurried past, on through the doorway at the back of the temple which mirrored the one at the front. It stood open to another green field that dipped down into a dell, this one full of foxtails and wildflowers and beasts. Cows, goats, and sheep grazed together, and a few black, bristly pigs rootled in the mud down at the far end. After searching for a minute, Taryn found Nel, grazing alongside two small fat ponies. His slash had become a thin white line.

She walked toward him, feeling strange and unsure. After a few paces, a brown girl stood up out of the tall grass in front of her. She wore a long slip that would have been white if it weren't stained with dirt and plant matter.

Who are you? she demanded, speaking the strange language that Taryn knew and hurt for knowing. The words refused to shape themselves in her head the way those of the fairies or goblins did. *You can't just let your horse go without taking off his tack!*

Taryn stopped and looked at the indignant girl, who she realized with some embarrassment was only short, not a child. Her dark hair billowed around her in dense curls.

He was determined to see the temple, she responded, trying to pull the sounds closer, make them more comfortable to speak. *He didn't give us time to take off his saddle.* Then, unsure, *His name is Nel.*

He's a fine horse, the girl—the young woman—said, watching her closely. Her words felt a little less strange, and Taryn found herself breathing deeply, letting the language slide over her instead of digging into her flesh. We don't see such fine horses in these parts, so far from the capital.

And who are you? she asked, ready to start the dance of oh-so-delicately refusing to give each other their names, while hinting broadly at their allegiances and their allies—

"It's Bo," the woman said. "I'm the priest."

"Oh—uh—well—"

Nel chose this moment to trot up and stick his nose into the ear of the curly-haired Bo. The two fat ponies followed determinedly.

"Nel here says your name is Taryn," she said, her voice disapproving. "That's a bad name. That's a name that will get you in trouble."

"What?" Taryn asked, bewildered. "Because you can use it to bind me?" Then, after the first sentence the priest had said sunk in, "You can talk to horses?"

"No, I talk to cows—it's part of the priest job—cows being sacred to *themself* in there—but sometimes a horse gets through. Common concern and all. That's the queen's name, and she doesn't care for anyone to share it. She sent out an edict when she was

crowned that all the girl-children who had been named after her
when she was born were to be renamed and never speak it again,
unless they meant to refer to her, under pain of whipping or having
their ears cut off." She considered Taryn thoughtfully as she
vigorously scratched under Nel's chin. "Of course, they *weren't* all
named after her, as it's an old name, and a common one."

"She doesn't sound like a very good queen," Taryn said.

"You'd be wise not to say so," the priest said. "Though you'd
be right. I'm only the priest here because the old priest is in prison
—or dead, which is more likely."

Taryn thought of Ash, lying white-faced back in the clearing
in the scrubby little wood, and wondered if all their magic was
enough to protect the three of them from an angry queen while
they searched for Oberon's daughter. *His real daughter.* Her stomach
hurt.

Taryn had been a common name, the priest said.

She was a queen because she had married a king; but whose
daughter had she been, before?

She knew—almost—and she didn't want to know.

Bo frowned at Nel, who lipped her hair. "Stop that, you. Nel
says he's sorry for almost throwing you. He saw how you looked
after his herdmate, and he's grateful. He knows you're not really one
of them that make him itch so—one of who?"

Taryn only shook her head.

"Where are you from, after all?" she asked. "You sound like
you're from here—maybe closer to the capital, even—and you look
like you're from here, with your coloring, but you don't know about
the queen?"

"I guess I've been living under a hill," Taryn said, trying and
failing to smile.

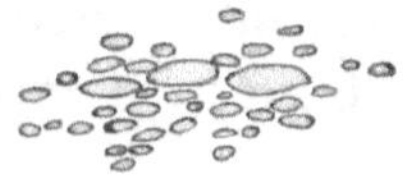

When Taryn and the goblin king returned to the camp, Nel
walking between them laden with packs full of bread, bacon, hard
cheese, and canteens of beer, Ash was sitting up next to the remains

of the fire. They stared into the middle distance. Lilith was nowhere to be seen, but the loud sounds of branches breaking emanated from the general direction of the stream.

Their face was still drawn and sallow, but their eyes focused. When Taryn dropped to her knees next to them and pressed her hand against their cheek, it was warm, only warm, not the terrifying chill of last night or the yet more frightening burn of infection.

"What," they said, turning toward her, a wan smile across their face. "You'd think you'd seen a ghost."

Taryn put her arms around Ash, unthinking, but jolted away when she touched their right arm. There was no sign of the splint she had helped the king make.

"What's happened?" she asked. "Your arm—"

"It's all right," the witch said, slowly raising the limb in question, fingers spread, and then dropping it again to touch their nose. There was no evidence of any breaks. "See."

Taryn sat back on her heels, blood rushing to her face in both relief and anger. "What *happened*," she repeated, her voice tight. "You were so badly hurt. I thought—any human with those injuries would have died."

"Not so bad as all that," Ash said, before looking into her face and understanding that the words lay on top of another, more important question. They looked back toward the king, a deep divot between their eyebrows. "Didn't you tell her—didn't you explain— about my—about how—didn't you tell her not to worry?"

"I tried," the king said. He had taken Nel's packs off during this exchange and was now busily rubbing the horse down, an activity Nel embraced in near-ecstasy, leaning against the king and drooling with enthusiasm. The king would not quite look at Ash.

"You must not have tried very hard," they said.

"Then *you* try," Taryn said, tears burning in the corners of her eyes. "I'd like to feel like less a fool right now, please."

"You aren't a fool. I only—" Ash looked deep into her face, a panicked, searching look in their pale eyes. "All witches have a patchwork of magic—things found, things given, things learned, things bought," they said finally. "I gave some things up. And I bargained for—other things."

"So you—you heal very fast," Taryn said, carefully. "Why didn't you tell me?"

"Faster than usual, this time around," Ash said, cheerful, before sobering. "It's not a good story. I'm not proud of what I gave."

"So we wasted our time, last night," she forced on.

"No," Ash said. "Well. I would have been all right, in a few days, but usually if I break something, it heals up crooked, and I have to break it again a couple times to get it right."

Taryn's mind was suddenly filled with the vision of Ash, white-faced and barely conscious, sweating and retching in the shadowy grass. "And you let them do that?" she demanded of the king.

"I—" he started.

"I don't need looking after," Ash interjected, with uncharacteristic sternness. Seeing Taryn's expression, their voice softened. "I've gotten on well enough by myself for eleven years, and I held up my end before that. You've no need to worry." They punctuated their point by lurching to their feet, only to stagger and tip to one side. Taryn rose too and hastily wrapped an arm about their waist, trying to steady them, but Ash must have weighed nearly twice as much as she did, and she stumbled too.

Suddenly the king was there, on the other side of the witch, an arm hooked beneath their armpits. Ash did not stagger. After a minute the king's grip slackened, and he stepped away.

"Thanks," muttered Ash, swiping the beads of sweat from their forehead with the back of one hand.

Taryn, her arm still tight around Ash's midsection, looked over their head at the king. He was staring at the witch, a look of terrible sorrow creasing his face.

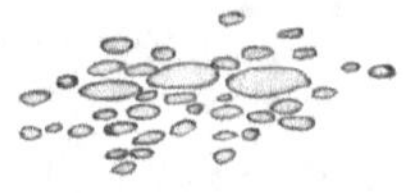

The three of them set out again at nightfall. This time Taryn rode in front of the king on Lilith. Ash went a little ahead on Nel.

Taryn suspected that anyone who looked out their window this night at the sound of passing hoofbeats would see only a normal rider on a normal horse, followed by a strange, massive shadow.

They swept through the village where the king had purchased supplies and Taryn had spoken with the priest. In the glimmer of moonlight, Taryn could finally make out the shape of the standard in front of the temple: a golden cow's head, capped by great, upward-curving horns. Ash made an odd sort of gesture toward the standard and bowed in their saddle. Taryn thought she heard the lowing of cattle from the meadow beyond in response.

They would ride to the capital city, the king had explained as the sun set. He was sure he knew where Oberon's daughter was. It was three weeks' travel on foot from the kingdom's far northwestern corner, where they had emerged from the woods, to this city, which sat just south of the river that cut the kingdom in two halves. The king said that riding Nel and Lilith, they should make it in three nights.

Taryn had her own suspicions, which bubbled up into her chest as something like panic. The closer they rode to the city, the more the surroundings became achingly familiar. But when she tried, as a sort of half-experiment, to imagine what sort of parents she *might* have had—if, just if, Oberon *might* not have been her father—what those parents *might* have been like—her mind presented her, not with a black boulder, but a flat, unapproachable nothingness. There had been nothing before Oberon. There was nothing after Oberon. This was not like the forgetting in Ash's forest, when she had known the size and shape of the thing that was missing, but a complete blankness. It was very hard for Taryn to breathe, even when Lilith slowed enough that the wind of her running didn't whip the air from her mouth.

At the end of the first night of running, they were still in wild enough country that when the day broke, Nel led them along a dry streambed away from the road and up across a stony bluff. He took them into the shelter of a circle of standing stones, hidden among the more natural rock formations.

"Is it safe?" the king wanted to know, pulling Lilith's nose back before she trotted through the entrance gap.

Ash looked up at the fingers of red light reaching across the sky. "Not sure. It's a good place to stop, if we can manage it. There's enough magic tied down here to confuse anyone who's looking." They slid down off Nel and walked a wide circle inside the stones, letting their hand pass over across their flat inner surfaces. A few faint sparks flew from their fingers.

"It's old and fair tired," the witch called to them. "Shouldn't take more than a few drops to appease it for a day's quiet."

They unsheathed a small knife, but the king urged Lilith forward into the circle. "I'll do it, then." He swung himself off onto the ground, but Taryn followed him so quickly he had to catch her.

"I know how to do a blood offering," she said, and did not add, Fairies love blood. "Let me." She caught Ash around the wrist that held the blade.

The witch looked at Taryn, then at the king, then down at the knife, then back at both of them. "Ah—well—"

"It's more than a few drops, isn't it," the king said.

In the end each of them sliced their palm and let it drip over the curdled lump of granite that marked the center of the circle. Nel tried to jab his nose on a sharp bush that was growing between two rocks so he, too, could contribute, but Ash caught his head and murmured to him until he gave it up. Lilith could not roll her eyes, so instead she kicked clods of dirt at each of them.

They slept wrapped together as the rising sun dried the dew on the grass around them. After some shifting and grumbling, Taryn turned to press her legs against the backs of Ash's thighs, and the king did the same to her. When she woke, she found that she had insinuated one arm beneath Ash's and thrown back the other to grip the rags of the king's tunic.

As soon as the sun set, they rode on. The number of villages and proper towns they passed through in the dark increased. Taryn, her mind full of frightening scenarios, went rigid every time Lilith's hooves suddenly rang out against cobbles. What would happen to them if they were stopped? The king said nothing, but the arm that rested on the pommel of the saddle curled back around her, and he stroked her stomach through her clothes.

They were never stopped, though more than one set of

curtains rustled open to watch their progress. By the time the sky started to lighten, the land was no longer broken by sporadic stretches of wilderness and was dense with houses, small farms, roadside shrines, and wells.

Ash clicked at Nel, and he slowed to a trot and then a walk which led him to one of these wells. It had a long stone trough where the water ran before pouring out onto the ground, and he stuck his nose in it and drank greedily.

"What say you?" they asked the king. "I can't be sure, but it looks like we're close to Joring, doesn't it?"

"There was the wizards' inn in Joring," he said thoughtfully. "They won't like Lilith, but they won't ask questions about her."

They turned off the main road shortly after, and by the time the sun was fully visible over the horizon they were standing in the high-walled courtyard of a prosperous-looking inn. A second-floor gallery built of wood ran around the inside of the building. A hosteler dressed in black leather silently took the king's proffered coins and led away the two horses, and another led them up an external staircase to their room.

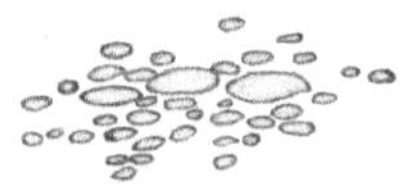

Taryn woke sticky from a nightmare. She lay rigid and silent as her eyes tracked around the room.

The wizards' inn was fine but plain. The curtains around the bed were clean, undyed wool. The stone walls were plastered, and an icon of the two-personed cow god hung on one wall. Rays of light slanted in through the shutters, painting bars of light on the rug.

The room did not look anything like the labyrinthine hallways of her dream, where Oberon and his many-jointed relatives crawled over the ceiling vaults and hid behind jeweled doorways, and an unknown great insect sat on a throne and called to her.

"All right?" Ash muttered from beside her. Taryn rolled over so that her nose was only an inch from theirs. They blinked at her sleepily.

83

"I'm not sure." She shivered involuntarily. "I feel like someone's watching me."

"Someone almost certainly is. For anyone who's looking, we're a great glowing mess," the witch said, yawning. "We're just hoping to get where we're going before any of those people figure out what to do about us."

Taryn had fallen onto the bed and gone to sleep as soon as the door of the room had closed, but Ash must have taken a few minutes to wash. When she breathed in through her nose, they smelled of plants and soap. Her heart slowed down, and she took another deep breath: sage, juniper. Without thinking she nuzzled into their neck and put her hand underneath their shirt to touch their skin.

"Ah," they said.

"I want to," she mumbled into the space under their jaw.

"But—"

"Do you not?"

"I don't think what I want is very relevant," the witch said thickly, as Taryn began to nibble on their collarbone.

She kissed their jaw, then the side of their mouth. "It is."

Ash went very still, their eyes focusing somewhere behind Taryn.

For what felt like several hours she refused to turn her head. She could feel Ash's heart hammering under her hand.

Taryn finally twisted her head to look over her shoulder, and met the many-lighted eyes of the goblin king. He sat in the room's only chair, slouched, his eyes intent on them both. His claws and tusks had come back.

Taryn felt Ash sit up. "I'll go check on Nel, shall I?"

"*No*," she said, furious. She was almost shocked out of her fury when her mind registered that she had not spoken alone but was accompanied by the king's much deeper voice. "No."

Ash looked down at her and, almost absently, laid a broad hand across where hers still rested on their chest. They let their hand drop and looked toward the shuttered window. "You don't owe me anything, you know."

"I do," the king said, at the same moment that Taryn said,

"It isn't about *owing*."

"No?" they asked.

"I looked for you every night after you disappeared," the king said. "I asked Ildar to make me a wolf so I could smell the magic I couldn't see, and so I could run through world-walls that might stop a goblin." He rose from the chair and came to stand by the bed.

"But—I failed," the witch said, sounding panicked. Their face had gone frozen and strange. "At the end, I failed. You can't have—I left so you wouldn't need to have any more to do with me. I left so I wouldn't embarrass you any more."

The king braced his hands on the bed, his fingers brushing Taryn's side. "You remember things very differently than I do."

Taryn, a little seed of triumph blooming in her gut, turned back to Ash and wrapped both arms tightly around them. The bed dipped a bit as the king laid himself down at her back.

"Then—we—her, yes?" the witch sputtered.

"Yes," Taryn said, kissing their neck.

The king laughed, before he slid both hands down Taryn's sides and then up again, pulling her tunic up. He wrestled with her for a minute—she didn't particularly want to let go of Ash, even for a few seconds—beyond he pulled the garment the way off and threw it to the end of the bed. She tried to take hold of the witch again, but the king pinned her hands over her head, against the mattress.

Ash looked at her face, hesitating, anxious; Taryn grinned and leaned forward to kiss them. She started to bite their lower lip, but the king tangled his other hand in her hair and pulled her head back.

The witch licked their lips thoughtfully. They lightly bit her chin, then her cheekbones, then her ears. Their hands moved over her bare torso in exploratory little circles, as if the witch needed reassurance that she was still real, still here. Their touch grew firmer, and they rubbed their knuckles into her lower back, and then her belly. They stroked a fingertip lightly over her ribcage until she thrashed with the ticklishness of it. Finally they took firm hold of her breasts, one in each hand, fingers gripping the soft flesh and thumbs circling the tips.

Taryn gasped and laughed and strained forward, wanting to kiss or bite or do something that would make them feel as much as she was feeling, but the king loosened his hand from her hair and then put it to her throat, pulling her head to the side so that he could kiss her jawline and her mouth.

It was enough to make her dizzy with sensation—with pleasure—with something very close to joy, as Ash moved one of their hands low on her belly and then between her legs. The king helped by pushing his knee between hers, lifting her leg to make a space for the questing hand to rest. Her whole body pulsed, and it felt like the two bodies next to her beat in the same rhythm. The king had started to massage the wrists he still held against the mattress.

"Is it well?" Ash asked, voice soft.

Taryn said something garbled, her mind too focused on the touch of skin on skin and the anticipation of what came next to form words, and the king moved his hand from her throat to her hip, where he rubbed large circles with his palm. Her head came to rest again on the mattress, her eyes locked with Ash's. They stroked her breastbone, watching, quiet, until she smiled again.

The hand between her legs began to rub, first lightly, up and around. Taryn's breaths came faster, in gasps. Ash had gone back to teasing one of her breasts, and the king followed suit and played with the other. Her eyes wouldn't quite focus.

Ash stopped moving their hand and pressed in, hard, with the heel of their hand.

"No—keep—" Taryn choked out.

"Wait," the king said in her ear.

Taryn did not want to wait; she tried to work her hips against Ash's hand, but they stilled her. The king pulled away from her back, and she almost cried out—what was he *doing*—

Suddenly he was pushing inside her. A moment later Ash was stroking her again, slowly, as the king worked his way deeper from behind. Taryn breathed in deeply. The king gripped her waist with both hands; she could feel his claws digging into her skin. The witch kissed her neck again, then her mouth, their hand rubbing faster. The king thrust deep inside her, again and again.

It was very hard to breathe; her whole body felt tight and desperate and ready. She was pushing up against a hard edge—but *there*—

Taryn would have cried out, but Ash pressed their fingers against her lips and the king wrapped one of his hands on top of that. She felt like she had perhaps exploded or suddenly turned into a gust of vapor and was now drifting through the air, slowly sinking into a great, quiet depth.

PART THREE

They were met by a contingent of the queen's soldiers where the road to Joring met the main road into the capital city. The sun had only just set; the goblin king had insisted they leave early enough to be in a full gallop south by the time darkness fell.

The soldiers, all mounted, had strung their horses across the road to make a loose blockade. The animals were uneasy, tossing their heads and stamping their feet. Taryn, who had taken it for granted that aside from Lilith, the goblin king's horses were more or less ordinary beasts, was shocked to see how small and drab these creatures were. Even in the dim twilight, Nel shone gold and red in comparison.

Lilith simply disappeared. A moment earlier Taryn and the king had both been mounted; now they were walking alongside Nel and Ash as though they'd come all the way from Joring that way. The king looked—well, he didn't look particularly human, but he didn't have his tusks or his crest, and his hands were jammed firmly into pockets that his coat hadn't had a few minutes ago.

Ash sighed and pressed a knee against Nel, who stepped forward. His ears were rigidly upright, and his skin quivered. The look in his usually-gentle eyes was positively murderous.

"What can we do for you, my good sirs?" they called.

The captain of the unit, to guess by the slightly finer cut of his jacket and the slightly taller horse he rode on, exchanged looks with the soldiers on his left and his right before kneeing his horse forward to meet them. He wore a black helmet with a visor that blocked most of his face from sight, and something about the dark eyes visible above the metal made Taryn's stomach churn.

His voice was clear and sonorous, perhaps to compensate for the visor. "I have a warrant for the arrest of the witch Ashmallen and all those who accompany the witch, for illegal and immoral use of magic."

"By whose authority is it granted?"

"Her Royal Majesty, the Queen Taryn Ardloch; Guardian of the Holy Cattle; Honorer of the Gods—"

"And what are the terms of the arrest?"

"To be carried out immediately," the captain said, and too late Taryn realized that six of the horsemen behind him carried short-bows that they had kept low at their sides. He gestured them forward with an impatient hand, and the soldiers drew up their bows, a pair of them taking aim at each of them—

"No," said the king. "I think not."

Everything went slow and sticky, as if the entire scene had been dumped into a bowl of jelly. The captain started to open his mouth, clearly meaning to shout, but got caught halfway, unable to move his jaw any further. The arrows that the bowmen had nocked to their strings slowed their flight and then fell to the ground.

The king crouched and then sprang up, landing on the great granite stone that marked the crossing.

"Know ye of goblins?" he asked in a strange voice, which sounded as though thousands of other voices spoke with him. "Traveled ye so far without us that we have been forgotten?"

He was a huge, terrible shadow atop the rock, both himself and many other goblin kings before him, none of whom had been half-human or made human bargains. Dozens or maybe hundreds of other shapes distorted and fought inside his shape: goblins and terrible creatures from the depths of the earth and perhaps even gods who made up his father's bloodline. Taryn, for a moment, saw what the soldiers saw, not a king who had chosen the open air and horses of his mother, but an apparition from somewhere in the far-away past, something that lived in the dark places of mountains and waited.

A fit king for the daughter of Oberon, she thought, her hands going slightly numb. Not intended for a human made of regular meat and blood.

The slow-spell cracked, and the soldiers' horses went wild, screaming and bucking, before spinning and pelting away from the crossroads as fast as their hooves could carry them. At the same moment, the king leaped from the stone, colliding solidly with the captain and knocking him from his horse to the ground. His mount wasted no time in following its companions down the road and away.

It was now too dark to see anything clearly, and the moon had not yet risen. A slithering sound indicated Ash dismounting, and Taryn felt them bump by her gently, pausing to tap her hand.

"You'd better not have killed him," they called forward to the king.

"I haven't," he said, and his voice was its normal baritone, with no vast genealogical undertones. "He's still breathing. He hasn't even knocked his head."

"A little light, dear one," Ash whispered.

Taryn, reassured by their low voice and embarrassed to need reassurance, hurried forward to stand beside them. She whispered the light charm, and the word floated out of her mouth as a small glowing ball.

It illuminated the face of the captain, from whom the goblin king had stripped the helm. The captain had black hair, heavy eyebrows, and an aquiline nose. His face was rather thin, and his eyes would have been cold if they hadn't been filled with terror. He might have been about forty.

Taryn stared at him. What had been an uncomfortable premonition when she saw only his eyes had now solidified into a memory, and it was not a good one. The last time she had seen this man, she had been much shorter, and he had leaned over her with a characteristically frigid smile. His dark hair was twisted and messy now, but then it had been perfectly combed and lustrous. He had worn a black silk doublet with expensive lace around the collar.

Someone small had been sitting behind her.

"It is good, at the very least," this man lying on the ground before her had said, "that our future queen will not fat and stupid."

The small someone behind her had started to cry, and then the memory ended.

She could not say how she knew this memory came from the same place that her knowledge of the language of this country spoke, from before the gray, confusing time spent in Oberon's court, when a wall had been erected in her mind to block off all that had gone before.

It filled her with revulsion. She wanted to step on his face, to crush his head in, or to ask the king—her king!—to bite his head off. She would offer up his bones to Ash to use in their fence.

"His name is Eradelior," she said, and the spasm of his face when she pronounced this made her certain this, too, was a true memory. "He is—of this country's nobility." This fact fell out of her brain like a bandage off an oozing wound.

"Excellent," Ash said. "I'm sure he has information for us."

"I will tell you nothing," he cried out suddenly, though Taryn doubted he understood the speech of goblins and witches. "I am loyal to my queen."

"I've no doubt you are," Taryn said, in the same language, and for the first time he really looked at her. His eyes bulged, and he compulsively started to make a gesture against evil against his chest. "Witch," he spat, though the word was barely comprehensible in his fear. "Wicked magic user. Fairy impostor. How dare you use the face of Her Majesty?"

"How dare she use mine?" Taryn snarled, while thinking, I *am* a witch. Nothing like Ash, but I was under the hill long enough that I know how to make things happen when I need them to happen. How can I go back to being someone who is perfectly human, perfectly unmagical?

The rest of what he had said caught up with her brain, and her stomach sank. She looked at Ash and the king. They know, she thought, and I know, and now we have to go face a queen who should have been me. I wish I could do almost anything else.

The man had gone very still and, if possible, looked even

more fearful than before.

The goblin king had followed this exchange with keen interest, one clawed hand still at the captain's throat, and one bare clawed foot planted on his chest. Now he looked up at Taryn. "What was he like—*before?* Would he have accepted a changeling queen if he knew her to be false?"

"For a copper penny and a spoonful of butter," Taryn said, bitter that she could not remember the face of the person who had said that phrase to her. It had been a kinder face.

"If he turned once, he can turn again," Ash said cheerfully. "His name is mud anyway, because he was sent to kill us—or at least seriously inconvenience us—and he failed. Help me truss him up and throw him up on Nel, and I'll find out how one gets into the queen's house while we ride."

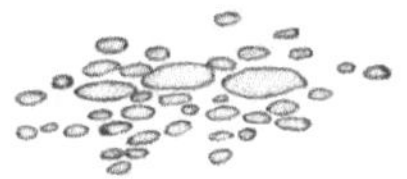

Taryn rode in silence for most of the night. The wind picked up, and every so often it carried a few words over from Ash questioning Eradelior: "gate," "how many", "soldiers," "temple." Once she thought she heard the word "cows" followed by a question— "how big did you say?" His wrists had been lashed to the pommel, and they sat behind him. She didn't see a knife in Ash's hand but felt sure it was there.

Her mind ached as though it were an overstuffed bag, creaking and shredding at the seams. When she tried to remember more about where she had been when Eradelior had spoken to her, a gray haze intruded. Everything became muggy and unclear inside her head. She looked just like the queen, Taryn reminded herself, and had her name too. What had that felt like from the inside? The captain had been wearing fine lace in the memory. If she stretched her mind as far as it could possibly go, pressing back the grayness with all her strength, she could just see her own hands, smaller and more slender than they were now, with lace at her wrists.

When she tried to turn her head in the memory, to look at

the small someone crying behind her, her head exploded with pain.

Taryn jerked back against the king's shoulder. The sky had started to go light, and the shadows of buildings rose on both sides of the road. Not yet visible at the end of the road was a massive gate that would open at sunrise into the city proper. The light would strike across the pale limestone of the walls and the dark wood of the door as was slowly cranked opened. She could not see it, but she knew it was there, and she stared ahead in misery. Above that gate, the city climbed successive terraces, until it reached a curtain wall wrapping the crest of the hill. There was a palace and the grandest temple of the two-bodied cow god in the whole country.

Taryn couldn't think of that anymore. Her head ached like someone was pounding nails into it.

"Why—" she started, hoping the words would push back the shadows in her head. "For what do you revenge yourself upon Oberon and his — his true daughter?"

The king did not answer for a long time but instead moved his hand against her belly in a slow circle. At first Taryn could not bear this—how could he think to offer comfort *now*, when everything was about to shatter into pieces no one could put back together?—but after a few minutes she felt her body relax.

"The sister," floated her way from atop Nel's back. She went rigid again.

"He did something to Ash," the king said.

"What did he do?" she asked, but there was no answer.

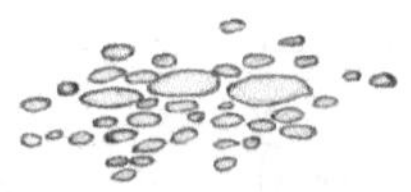

Based on Eradelior's knowledge, they passed through the great gate but then turned off the main thoroughfare into a narrow street lined with narrow houses. Lilith vanished again as soon as the gate came into view, leaving the king and Taryn to walk up the steep hill after Nel and his two riders. She wondered if this was Lilith's own magic, or a result of the charm that Ash had made for the king.

"He says there's a small door in the east wall of the palace, where hay and oats are delivered for the god's cattle," Ash relayed.

Taryn looked sharply at Eradelior, but he would not meet her eyes. She waited a moment, and the nugget of a memory coalesced. "That's the priest-door. They're sure to see us for what we are and stop us," she hissed.

"Recall what I said would happen for every lie you tell," Ash said to the soldier. "Is it safe for us to go through this door?"

"The priests have been restricted to the holy fields in the center of the palace," Eradelior said, sweat visible on his upper lip and forehead. "They are no longer allowed to meet with the grain merchants themselves."

"Keeps them from passing messages about how bad it is inside, I expect," Ash said. "Very well, then."

They walked up a series of crooked and shadowy streets, always climbing higher. Taryn wondered what threat Ash had made to so terrify Eradelior.

The walls of the palace were thicker even than the walls of the city close, built of darker and older stone. It had been here far longer than the city surrounding it on all sides, when the rulers of this country had feared armies from without more than traitors from within. The houses and shops stopped a full furlong from the walls, though the deep ditch that had once surrounded them had been filled in and covered over with turf. Taryn felt uncomfortably exposed standing in the open. The priest-door was larger than she remembered, tall and wide enough to admit a small cart.

There were no soldiers in sight, though the towers at either side of the door had arrow-slits just above head height.

"Order them to open the door," the goblin king said to Eradelior, gripping his foot.

"They'll see I'm bound," the captain responded, an edge of panic to his voice. "They won't follow my word. They'll shoot us."

"You'd be surprised," Ash said. "Nothing makes a human so easy to fool as living under a fairy glamour for years and years."

"But—"

"Do it," said the king.

Eradelior called to the guards in the towers. They responded with no hint of suspicion, and when they ratcheted open the door, two of them even descended to bow to him and clang the butts of their spears against the ground. The expression on his face, as he realized that they truly could see no more than Ash wanted them to see, was something to behold, Taryn thought.

The priest-door opened into a steep cobbled way that twined around the back of the palace. Within the walls, the palace sat on a wide, flat terrace at the front of the enclosure, looking down over the city; the great temple sat at the back, just behind the crest of the hill where the sacred herd grazed. In the uncertain before, Taryn thought that she had been here and looked down on the priest-road from somewhere up on the terrace. It seemed to her that then—then there had been a constant flow of traffic into and out of this door—priests from other parts of the country, grain, hay, veterinary students, worshipers seeking blessing for themselves or their families or their cows. Now the road had gone weedy with disuse.

Her head continued to ache ferociously. They'd have to go up through the temple and then descend down the causeway that led into the queen's throne room, where she would have to speak to the other Taryn—the false Taryn. The real daughter of Oberon.

The cobblestone way delivered them into a side courtyard of the great temple, a sunken stone area with great pulleys suspended overhead on moving wooden arms to heave hay and grain up into the storage mows. Rust outlined each mechanism. Taryn stared upward, her heart sinking.

The witch had dismounted, leaving Eradelior tied to the saddle. Nel was not entirely happy with this arrangement, and he kept swerving toward nearby walls and half-rearing.

A long ramp led up the side of the courtyard into the temple. It was, as Bo's sanctuary had been, a very large barn, though in this case the great span of the roof was held up inside by rows of stone columns. But there was no decoration, nothing to distract from the dust suspended in the sunlight falling through small holes in the roof. Taryn wasn't sure if this bareness was to honor the two-bodied god or if the great temple, too, was falling out of use. It was empty and silent, and she didn't think it had been before. A few dark figures hurried away from them behind the columns.

The end of each wing of the temple was open to the pasture beyond. Framed in one of these openings was a Cow.

The gray space around Taryn's memories had allowed through a vague knowledge of the holy cattle of the great temple, but it had not prepared her to be confronted by a massive, red-dappled beast, as tall as Nel at the shoulder, its eyes huge and dark and knowing. Its head was crowned with a pair of horns as tall again as the cow herself, each one so wide that Taryn could not have wrapped her two hands around its base.

The cow, who had been scratching her side on the edge of the great open door, stopped and stretched out an inquisitive nose toward them. She wore a heavy collar hung with a bronze bell, and as she walked toward them it clanged with thunderous reverberations around the empty building.

Taryn went to meet the cow, her hands outstretched.

Behind her they were talking. "Oh, what a *beauty*" —that was Ash, of course, and if she had not been entirely focused on the beast in front of her she would have laughed— "You must not touch the god's cattle!" —that was Eradelior, with terror in his voice — "Take care," said the king, his voice low, worried, "you don't know her."

The cow stopped, stiff-legged, a few paces away. She sniffed Taryn's hand, rolling a skeptical eye in her direction. Something like a question felt like it was shaping itself in the sunlit dust. *Who are you,* maybe, or *why do you smell so strange—*

And then the question broke and dissolved back into the air, because a new figure appeared in the outer door, silhouetted against the bright green of the pasture outside. The person paused for a moment, squinting into the darkness of the temple, before plowing forward.

"There you are, Pumpkin, you monster. I'm sure you think you're very funny; Leli has been hunting for you all over the south paddock." The figure came closer and resolved into a tall, broad-shouldered young woman wearing the priest's plain white shift. A great mass of dark hair fell in a braid down her back. She was fat in the way that farmwives who can carry a young hog under each arm are often fat, softness layered over heavy muscle.

Taryn stared unhappily at the young woman's heavy brows and arched nose and rather delicate chin; it was rather like staring into a sunburned and rounder version of her own face.

"Here, Pumpkin," the young woman said, before she met Taryn's eyes and stopped. Her face froze and then went hard, and her gaze went to the floor and stayed there.

"How . . . *unusual* . . . to see you in the temple, your Majesty," she said, and her voice had gone flat and tinny. "I did not think you cared for the smell of livestock." Her eyes seemed to skim over Ash and the goblin king before landing on Eradelior. An emotion akin to hatred kindled in her eyes, but her face did not move. "Nor your . . . lieutenant."

"I greet thee, your holiness," Eradelior said. In spite of being bound on a horse between two people who were likely to kill him quite soon, it seemed his contempt for the young woman was so ingrained that he could not contain it. "But surely my lady Elsyn must greet her *sister* as befits her dignity."

The young woman's face had gone beyond frozen to utterly rigid. She executed a small, stiff bow in Taryn's direction, before looping an elbow around one of Pumpkin's horns and hauling her head toward the door. "By your leave, I would return to my duties."

She turned away from them, dragging a complaining Pumpkin out of the temple and into the sunlight.

Taryn found her voice. "Elsyn?"

The young woman paused, but then she continued on outside as though she had not heard.

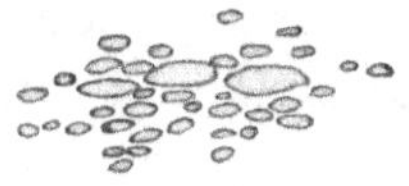

There had been another daughter, a better daughter.

There had been a daughter who couldn't be impersonated by a vicious fairy for eleven years without anyone knowing the difference. A daughter—a *sister*—she had left behind so completely that she had had no thought or memory of her for eleven years.

There were tears in her eyes, in her hair, soaking the collar of her tunic, in her nose and her throat. She couldn't begin to say what was most horrible; the sudden knowledge that the memory of Eradelior bending over her, murmuring hateful things, had been the last time anyone had come between Elsyn and the cruelty aimed at her; the violent little bursts of recollections of being a sister, of having a sister, of not being so terribly alone; or the horrible voids that were left. She still couldn't remember. *She couldn't remember.*

She had run out into the pasture after Elsyn, a garbled explanation in her mouth—*please understand, it wasn't my fault*—but she and Pumpkin had gone, disappearing behind one of innumerable green hillocks. Taryn was alone in a patch of browning grass, weeping. She sank down onto her knees and pressed her face into her hands, sobs shaking her whole body. It would have been better to have stayed in Oberon's court and have her whole body spun out like a ribbon, a voice whispered from inside the gray haze. At least then she wouldn't have known what she had lost.

When hands took hold of her, it was two pairs, one long and clawed and one broad and thick-fingered. The king pulled her shoulders up, away from the earth, until she lay back against him. Her raw eyes burned in the sunlight. Ash knelt beside her, one hand wrapped around hers and one holding a flagon of water to her mouth. The water was very cold, and she drank until it was empty.

She stared into nothing for a long time, as pain beat inside her body. Perhaps this is what it felt like to die, she thought. She certainly couldn't imagine going on like this.

"Did you *know?*" Taryn burst out, trying to sit up and almost falling over with light-headedness. "Is your revenge worth bringing me here for—for *this?*" She started to cry again. She felt like she might vomit.

Ash produced another flagon from their bottomless knapsack and a cloth, which they soaked and wrung out. They pressed it against her hot forehead, then her cheeks, then, lightly, tentatively, across her eyes.

"I didn't realize the memory would come back so suddenly and so strongly," the king said, and his voice rumbled against her back. "I had heard news of the princess here, and I thought it was strange, and stranger yet that her parents should die so young, right when she might be crowned. That the voices on the wind and the speech of the trees should say Oberon's daughter under the hill suddenly appeared young again, and dark—but I did not hear much of the sister, and I did not think of what that meant. I am sorry."

"As am I, though I'm sure it does little enough to hear me say so," Ash said wryly. "Do you need to eat something? I have some toast."

Taryn gasped involuntarily with laughter and then started to sob again. "When—when did you *make* it? Do you — do you—"

"Steady," Ash said, pressing on her belly until she exhaled. "Deep breath."

She inhaled partway, sobbed, tried again. The king bit her shoulder, lightly, through the cloth of her tunic. The sun was painfully bright.

"Do you have a toast rack in that bag?" she asked.

"I have many things in the bag," Ash said. The king laughed, and Taryn almost smiled.

Nel chose this moment to clomp over the top of the hillock and snuffle at the king's face.

Taryn did laugh at that, but she stopped when she saw Ash's grimace. "What is it?"

"I left Eradelior tied to Nel," they said. "Where's he gone?"

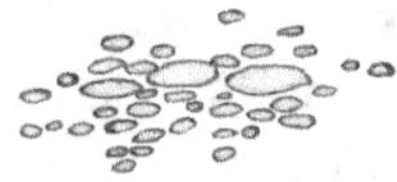

There was nothing left but to go to the throne room.

"If she's not there, we will wait for her," Ash said. "It's what she came here for, and it's what she will return to."

"You can be a queen without a palace," the goblin king, descendant of horse-lords, said.

"Not a fairy queen," Ash responded, at the same moment that Taryn said, "Not if you're Oberon's daughter."

The king went in front, leaping from hillock to hillock in the rolling pasture. He was almost fully goblin now, the powerful muscles of his hind legs launching him through the air like a great cat. Ash and Taryn followed him at a run. The holy field was massive, and soon Taryn was winded. Ash grabbed her hand, and the pain in her lungs subsided. Last came Nel at a subdued trot, his ears low, clearly ashamed that he had let his rider escape.

The causeway from the fields down to the oldest part of the palace was narrow, lined in massive, irregular, flat-faced stones, each speckled with orange and green lichen. The king ran along the tops of the stones, barely touching each one, but Taryn, Ash, and Nel slid across the crooked paving slabs. The sky, clear when they had stood in front of the temple, had gone dark. The wind speared down the causeway after them.

"She knows we're here," Ash shouted. Taryn clutched their hand tighter. Nel lifted his head and whinny-screamed at the roiling clouds.

The causeway bent halfway through its length, curving sharply to the right and down. The king hurtled around this bend without slowing, but a moment later a spear arced up above the stones, thrown at him by an unseen soldier. Taryn slowed; the king threw himself off the boundary stones. She heard screams.

Ash drew their knife and pressed another into her hand, but before either of them could turn the corner, Nel shouldered his way past them, trumpeting, his nostrils red and his eyes wild.

Three soldiers were down when they joined the king, and another four surrounded him and the horse. Taryn tried to remember how she had called up the illusions when they had passed through the lich-land, but Ash called out.

"Hold, hold fast." Two of the soldiers, tall men with lined faces, stopped and looked up at them, but suddenly the man behind them turned tail and ran, sprinting down the last hundred feet of the causeway. They whirled to follow him, and Ash moved faster than Taryn had ever seen them move before. They dove forward, seizing the leather tunics of both soldiers and dropping to the ground. The two men were of such an even height that their heads smacked together with an ominous *thud*. Ash cracked ankles and knees with the pommel of their knife, bringing the two of them tumbling down. Taryn ran forward—if only Ash wouldn't keep getting themself into places where she couldn't aim a blade safely—

The goblin king did something that made the man he was sitting on go perfectly white and still; he and Nel leaped together over the body and went pelting down the causeway after the escaped soldier.

Ash stood up from the now-unconscious soldiers. "I think they knew me," they said thoughtfully. "But we must go on, quickly—here—" They ran.

"Should they have?" Taryn asked, skidding after them. The causeway ended in a huge stone doorway, set partly into the hillside. There was no door, only a great, cool darkness emanating from within.

"Well, I recognized them," Ash murmured, putting out a hand to slow her. They touched two fingers to their lips.

The passage continued downward, a pale gray rectangle visible at its end. Ash cast an intent look back at Taryn, caught her hand, and squeezed it, before they walked side-by-side into the throne room.

It was as cavernous as the barn-temple, and as bare. The stone walls rose to an enormous height before arching to meet each other above. There were no windows, only a row of small round apertures in the ceiling and two great open oil lamps hanging on long chains from the vaults.

Taryn thought there might have been tapestries covering the walls, before. There certainly had been people, then, surrounding the stone dais at the center of the massive hall, the sounds of talking and feet shuffling and clothes rustling.

Now there was silence. Barely any light came through the punctures in the ceiling above, and the flames in the lamps cast a dim, flickering glow.

A single, low chair sat on the dais. The figure who sat upon it was darker than the shadows around it.

Where was the king? Where was Nel?

Taryn turned her head, and her heart jumped into her throat. Where was *Ash?* They had been here a minute ago, their hand lightly resting on hers, but now there was no one. She spun around. The doorway to the outside had gone; behind her was only smooth stone.

"What have you done?" she shouted and ran at the figure on the dais.

"What have you done?" it said back to her in her own voice.

Taryn lifted the knife Ash had given her, meaning to throw it, but the figure was suddenly in front of her, gripping her wrist, lifting it over her head.

Oberon's true daughter smiled at Taryn with Taryn's own mouth, Taryn's own teeth, Taryn's own eyes, running Taryn's own tongue over Taryn's own lips.

"Impostor," Taryn hissed.

"Impostor," the other repeated. *"I will not suffer an impostor to live."*

Taryn opened her mouth to answer back, but no sound came from her lips. Something invisible pressed against her throat and her tongue, and it took a great effort to breathe, let alone form words.

The throne room blurred into unreal, patchy darkness, like the shadows that had surrounded the lich-lights. This isn't quite real, Taryn thought. Fairies sometimes threw up a temporary hill underneath a farmhouse or a barrow or somewhere else they wished to haunt by burying a possessed stone and then running tunnels in from more established hills, but a fairy space only existed uneasily inside a human one. True fairy hills were hidden, unfindable by magic or map, but these shoddy hills let light and music leak out for weeks. Usually after whatever revel had been planned was over they collapsed in on themselves, sometimes leaving a hole that an unwary human might slip through.

Whatever mock throne room Oberon's daughter had made for herself could likely be shattered as well. She wished she had iron, or silver, or salt, or anything that could throw a fairy off her guard, but she had only the bronze knife Ash had given her. She had been under the fairy hill so long herself that she was not sure she could have held iron, silver, or salt without burning herself.

Taryn punched forward with her free hand, but the fairy caught her wrist and gripped it hard. What had the king said? *A changeling cannot stay in the same house with the child it has replaced.* Of course Oberon's daughter had found a loophole, making a place that was not the house inside the house.

Did the king and Ash know where she had gone, where the other daughter had taken her?

Oberon's daughter forced her knife hand behind her head. She wants me to cut my own throat, Taryn thought, furious.

She thought of Ash and jerked her head forward, meaning to crack her skull against that of the fake queen. But Oberon's daughter was not so human as that; her neck craned backward and kept craning until it was a long fleshy snake. Her grip on Taryn's wrists tightened. She seemed to have acquired more arms and legs beneath the shadowy dress she wore.

If only I could *see,* Taryn thought. The blade in her hand was pressing against the side of her neck now, and she could feel a thin trickle of blood running down her shoulder.

She spoke the light charm as an impulse, and a globe of light shot from her lips and bounced off the fairy's unearthly face. The other daughter jerked, and for a moment the features that had been schooled to such a careful likeness of Taryn's wavered.

Taryn shouted the charm again, again, again, balls of light falling from her mouth in a torrent. Some of them smacked against the fairy's shivering face, some fell and clung to her fleshy dress, some went soaring out into the not-real darkness—

Her grip slackened for a moment, and Taryn yanked the knife from her neck and hurled it away. Ash! she shouted, though the enchanted darkness swallowed up her words. My king! *I'm here! Come find me!*

She tore herself away, chanting the light charm as she ran down the endless length of the throne room toward the dais, which got smaller and farther away as she ran. As the syllables crushed one into another, the glowing bobbles poured from her lips in a long string. The sound of many clawed feet scuttling across the hard floor followed her.

Taryn seized the rope in both hands, pulling it arm's-length by arm's-length from her mouth, and spun to face the other daughter, Oberon's daughter, the would-be queen. She had grown much larger, with pale white arms emerging everywhere from her torso, all patting the folds and drapes of her shining garment, but she still wore Taryn's face. As she twisted, her shoulders became visible through the top of the dress, or exoskeleton, or whatever it was. Just above her right shoulder blade was a round mark, like a many-pointed star.

Taryn stared at this but did not have time to think about what it meant. She wound the rope of lights around her elbow, tying it off in a great loop before casting it up, up, over the mass of the other daughter, who now dove down toward her, her sharp-nailed fingers tense, ready to dig into her body. The rope got thinner and paler as it soared away from her, as though it might disintegrate before ever falling down around that sinuous, too-long neck.

The illusions she had used to distract the lich-lights did not come so easily this time; Taryn had to dig at her own clothes, ripping off bits of fluff and threads, and score her arms, filling the gap under her fingernails with skin and blood, to give herself enough material to work with. The illusion she blew upward as the other daughter's fingers sank into her shoulder was a single creature, a sort of folded darkness like a piece of cloth. It gusted upward, catching the light-rope on its wings and pulling it against the pale, ever-lengthening column of the neck. It spun like a toy in the air and wound the rope tight.

It was something to focus on, Taryn thought, besides the terrible, growing pain in her shoulder. She felt like she had been speared, not just grabbed by a set of too-sharp fingernails. Another hand pawed at her throat, and she shoved it away. Other hands were touching her, disgusting, creeping digits making her itch, but none had the force of the hand embedded in her muscle. Her shirt was growing damp where the fairy's fingers had penetrated her flesh.

The papery illusion crested upward and then floated gently across the ceiling and out through one of the skylights. For a moment the light-rope became taut, straining against the fairy's neck, and her stolen face shivered furiously—

Suddenly the room shifted. The stones sharpened, focused; the light coming in through the ceiling apertures strengthened. The fires in the great hanging lamps fizzled out.

The other daughter was Taryn's size again, her neck and hand restored to normal length and sharpness, reclining against the back of an ornate throne set on the dais at the center of the room. It was not anything like the real throne. The light-rope had become a set of glistening pearls around her throat. Taryn touched her shoulder; the rips in her skin were gone, though she thought she could feel something wet sticking the fabric of her shirt against her side.

The walls were still smooth and featureless on all sides, with no hint of a door leading in or out.

"I would be a better queen than you," the fairy said conversationally. "I was raised for this. I was *born* for this."

"As was I," Taryn said thickly. Her shoulder still hurt mightily, and she felt faint. "As was my sister."

"Your sister is nothing," the fairy spat. "A cow priest to a nothing-god. Covered in shit and milk."

"She will be queen over this country," Taryn shot back.

Her stomach twisted around itself, as she understood that her words were the truth. She understood, too, the truth that she had not spoken: she, Taryn, would not be returning here. The throne had been stolen from her, but she could not take it back. She had been gone too long, and she had changed too much. She had taken vows to serve another kingdom, another king.

Taryn smiled grimly. She would keep those vows, if she could get through this.

The other daughter leaned forward, her copied face a frozen mask. "What do you think you're laughing at?"

A fluttering shape caught the edge of Taryn's vision, though at first she thought it was a trick of her exhausted eyes. The kite-like illusion had come back in through a skylight behind the throne, looking for all the world like a piece of folded paper drifting downward on a draft of air.

"You," Taryn said, afraid the other daughter's attention would go toward the ceiling. Something denser, darker, more solid was in the process of coming through the hole after the illusion. "You're ridiculous. Your real father won't ever give up his throne, so your only chance to rule is to steal someone else's."

"He *helped* me," screamed other-Taryn. "He wanted me to be safe from that nasty goblin-king's vow." Now she smirked and chittered. "Thought he could steal away Oberon's daughter and make her hate him, did he! Now look what's happened! I *adore* my father, more than ever!"

But he did, Taryn thought, her heart sinking again. Foster daughter, fake daughter, but it would satisfy the letter of the promise.

She let her eyes flick upward for a moment. The thing that had followed the flying illusion struggled, wiggling one limb and then another through the skylight.

"Now look what's happened," she agreed. "You've been cornered far away from home and will pass into darkness without anyone ever knowing your real name."

The thing gathered itself up and forced itself through the skylight with an inaudible *pop* that Taryn felt in her jaw. It landed on the back of the hovering illusion, and they ghosted to the floor of the fake throne room together.

"This is *my territory*," the fairy said smugly. "I have made it and I have held it and it is *mine*."

"For how much longer?" Taryn asked.

The dark thing had become a figure, a short, broad-chested figure with pale skin and a shaven head. It walked to one wall of the throne room—the masonry tried to play the same trick of perspective that the throne had and slide away—but the figure reached out and stilled its movement. With the other hand it brought a silver-edged knife down into the stones, slicing them open as though they were a side of bacon or a big cheese. The wall opened.

Other-Taryn felt that, as surely as though she had been lacerated herself. She opened her mouth, and the resulting scream found its way into the roots of Taryn's teeth, her sinuses, the muscles around her intestines.

The fairy rushed at Ash in a buzz of wings and clatter of chitin-armored legs, her human form forgotten. "*I'll tell you what's funny!*" she howled. "*I'll tell you what's funny!*"

It seized the witch by the shoulders, hauling them upward and tearing their jacket. Taryn rushed forward, or tried to rush, but her body felt broken and old and slow. Ash would be all right, she told herself, Ash was always all right—

The fairy shook the witch, splitting the cloth of their jacket further. "See! *See here!*" They stabbed at the star-shaped freckle that she had seen on Ash's back that afternoon weeks ago—or had it been months? She felt like she had never not known Ash.

The hole in the wall shook and echoed with the sound of hooves. Taryn stumbled forward, almost falling, her heart hungry to see the goblin king—*her* king—but what burst from the stones was not Nel or Lilith, but another Cow, or rather COW. This beast was as much like Pumpkin, who they had seen in the great temple, as Pumpkin was to lesser bovines.

The fairy dropped Ash, who immediately crawled away, and slowly spun in the air to face this new threat.

The COW was red, brindled with black, both colors so deep they glowed. Her eyes were enormous and black, each one holding centuries of night sky. Her horns shone white and rose in great, lyre-shaped arcs over her head. The muscles of her haunches rippled as she paced toward them. She could have carried another cow on her shoulders without noticing, Taryn thought in awe.

The COW looked around the fairy's throne room, bellowed once, and then charged the Other-Taryn.

She should have been able to fly out of reach—Oberon's daughter had his beetle-veined wings—but she struggled upward as though a great weight hung from her body.

Then the COW's black-tipped horn pierced her heart.

She opened her mouth to scream, but her body blew apart as she did so, withering into a plume of dust.

Then everything around them shattered and fell to pieces.

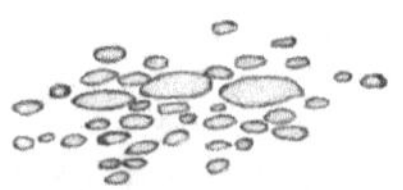

When Taryn woke, she was on the real floor of the real throne-room, and there were two faces peering down at her.

A third face tried to join them, but Ash shoved Nel's nose away.

"Are you back with us, dear one?" they asked.

She tried to sit up and was immediately assaulted by a cacophony of pain along her left side, where Oberon's daughter had grabbed her. She fell back, gasping, and realized she was lying across the king's knee's.

She wanted to pull them both down on top of her, and she hurt too much to move. She was sure she would feel grief later—she was sure she would be overwhelmed by the enormity of what she had just lost with such finality—but at this exact moment all she could muster was relief. Perhaps she had not won, but neither had Oberon's daughter.

"Are you all right?" the king asked, but before Taryn could begin to think how to answer that impossible question, a massive, wet nose shoved forcibly past his face. The shiny nose descended on Taryn's face, and a very long, pink tongue emerged from beneath it to explore her hair.

FINE, the COW said. JUST BRUISED.

She withdrew her huge nose and cast a skeptical dark eye down on Taryn. She forced herself to lift her head an inch so she could see just a little bit more, and found that Elsyn stood next to the cow, her hand on the high, humped back. She did not look at Taryn.

"The shadow you sent came up through a crack in the floor, and I followed it back down as best I could," Ash said. Taryn wanted to ask what had happened to Eradelior, or the escaped soldier, but she noticed smears of dried blood on the witch's tunic and on the hands that held her arm and decided not to. "*He* went back to the temple and found your sister, and she brought Bean with her."

The godly COW, whose name was apparently Bean, swung her massive head to survey the king. He stared back.

HORSE-LORD, the COW said to him. YOU ARE TOO FAR FROM YOUR HERD.

"I am very far from home," he said politely.

The COW turned her eyes to Ash. THE SMALL, WICKED COWS CRY FOR YOU. THEY WAIT IN THE WOOD. They all were regaled with an image of four goats clustered together under a tree, bleating pitifully.

"Are the—ah—regular-sized cows all right?" the witch asked anxiously.

THEY ARE FINE, said the COW. WE ARE ALWAYS FINE.

"Are we?" Elsyn asked, her voice half-cracking. It was the first thing she had said.

I AM BOSS COW, AND YOU WILL BE BOSS COW THROUGH ME, Bean said. WE WILL *MAKE* IT FINE.

"What about me?" Taryn asked. "I am not a boss cow." She tried to laugh, but it hurt so much that she settled for a racking cough. Ash muttered something and pressed now-cool hands against her bruised side.

NO.

"Then what am I?"

YOU HAVE TWO HERDS, the COW said impatiently. YOU FIGURE IT OUT.

This was apparently as much as she had to say on the subject. She wriggled her skin all over, as if she were shaking off a host of flies, and walked ponderously from the hall.

Elsyn at first made to go after her, then paused and looked back at them, then started to leave, then turned, planted her feet, squared her shoulders, and faced the three of them and Nel head-on.

"Things can't go on as they have been," she said, in a too-loud voice. "The only noble houses welcome in the city are those who brought—*her*—gold and things she liked and dripped flattery in her ears, like the beast Eradelior. Only the people who make the lives of those they are beholden to a misery." She took a deep breath. "That gold has not gone to roads, not to hospitals, not even to the army. It's all a shambles. We—the priests—there are so few of us left to do the work that needs doing, the legal work and the veterinary care. There was a cattle plague last year," she added, her voice cracking a little. "We've seen it before, we knew what could be done, but we weren't allowed to leave the temple compound. Thousands of beasts died."

She stopped, clearly stricken, and they waited.

"Any queen here would have few allies. *That one*—pushed away everyone who might have been able to stop her or—or help us," she said finally. "She *broke* everything."

The king spoke. "We will open the old road that once connected the lands of my father with those of your mothers," he said gravely.

"Goblins have never cared about what we—what humans do," Elsyn said.

"Your domain does not hold the sum of all humanity," Ash murmured. They shifted Taryn to place their cold hands against her aching back. Her side felt noticeably less painful already.

"We have cared about the humans who were our concern," the king said. "And you have become that." He paused, considering his next words. "You will have allies among those I will send to you, though they may not be the ones you looked for."

Elsyn looked down at Taryn. Her face was brown, from many years outside—how many? When had the false queen sent her out to live with the priests?—slashed across by heavy black brows drawn low over her dark eyes.

Taryn turned her earlier assessment around in her head. She's not a sturdier version of me, she thought. I'm a paler, less-real version of *her*. She wished she could hide her face in the king's clothes.

With some difficulty—and some help from the king and Ash, when they realized what she was trying to do—Taryn sat up. Whatever Ash had done had made her left shoulder and side of her torso go numb, which, while certainly an improvement, did not make it easy to move.

"Elsyn," she said. Her sister opened her mouth, clearly meaning to keep enumerating the damages done, but Taryn hurried on. "I, Taryn, commend the throne to you." Were those the right words? They had to be good enough. "I relinquish all right to rule here, forever, until my life ends."

This was clearly not what Elsyn had thought was going to happen. Her mouth opened and closed a few times before she found the words. "I'm a *priest*. The queen has never been a *priest*."

"Perhaps now is the time for there to be a first, then," Ash interjected. "You may not have friends among the noble houses, but the temples give you a network that touches every town in your country, no matter how small. And those holy ones who have stood by you through what has happened already—well."

Elsyn's mouth snapped shut, but she nodded, slowly.

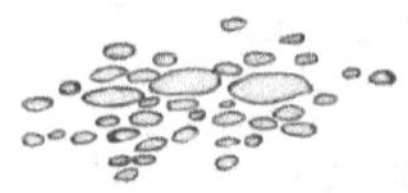

Taryn did not remember very much about the coronation. Of the three of them—five if she counted Nel and Lilith, who Ash told her was grazing with Bean and Pumpkin in the holy fields— only the king and Nel were known officially to be in the palace. Elsyn and the priests had provided him with new clothes of black leather and smooth black wool, and he cut a fine and imposing figure at the ceremony.

He was not the only goblin there. She did not know how a message had been sent to the goblins' castle, but four days after Oberon's daughter was destroyed, a contingent of the king's cousins entered the city, riding the most beautiful horses. Ildar, the horse-lord wizard, had opened the old road down from the mountains, and it had taken them hardly three days to get to the capital city. The goblin cousins made an imposing formation of riotous colors, pointed ears and bristling crests, tusks and claws, silver spears and curved swords, behind their somber king. Taryn hoped that any of the nobles who might have thought to acquire influence over a vulnerable new queen looked at her friends and thought twice.

Taryn was, officially speaking, dead. The story that had been put around, with the help of the priests of the high temple, was that fairies had tried to kidnap her by opening a tunnel into the throne room, and when she had run away from them she had fallen and broken her neck. The abrupt closing of the fairy tunnel, which Elsyn had sworn to witnessing with her own eyes, was the reason given for the lack of a body.

Her first order as the ascendant queen was to commission every active witch and priest to create defenses against fairy tunnels for their town or temple or farmstead.

There were not so many witches and priests left, after eleven years of Oberon's daughter, she told the goblin king grimly. But maybe there would be more soon.

Ashmallen the witch had an unusually unpleasant reputation among the queen's soldiers, which Ash did not explain and Taryn did not ask about. The soldiers they had knocked out had added their stories of being cursed by the witch to the cloud of ill reputation already around them, and the blame for the four soldiers the goblin king had killed—the three on the causeway, and the fourth, the runaway, who he had cornered in the throne room—had shifted seamlessly to them. The palace guard had set up dozens of extra checkpoints to scrutinize the hundreds of citizens who flooded the city for the coronation, searching for the witch and maybe even for fairies masquerading as humans, but they did not notice one extra small, gray, drab person staying in the temple, nor the small, drab, barely-visible shadow they held close to their side.

Eradelior had been found dead in a closet. He had been killed by magic, but no one was quite sure whose magic.

The coronation was a strange ceremony, made stranger by grief and uncertainty. Elsyn wore the headdress and white robes of a high priest, though Oberon's daughter had made sure she had never been promoted to such a lofty position. The headdress bore great curving golden horns, thankfully hollow. Elsyn, already a tall woman, had to hold the headdress in front of her to enter the throne room, before resettling it on her head. She had wanted the herd of sacred cattle to be part of the ceremony and come down into the throne room, but she settled for every priest left in the high temple, standing in white-clothed ranks behind the throne. There were about twenty of them, mostly women, all wearing horns as well.

There was some confusion about how to place the crown on Elsyn's head without disturbing the headdress. She had been adamant that her religious duties, to her herd and her fellow priests, would not be symbolically diminished in the ceremony. The crown was very old and simply made, a heavy band of gold inlaid with large red cabochons. It did not bend.

A handful of the most elevated nobles and senior priests fiddled with the crown for a long, awkward minute, while the gathered crowd of hundreds held their breath. Elsyn stood in front of the throne, shoulders squared, face schooled to a rigid expression. The throne room, for all its massive dimensions, felt stuffy and hot. Finally Ildar the wizard stepped forward, took the crown, and lifted it to Elsyn's brow. He did something no one could see, and when he took his hands away the crown had become part of the golden headdress, welded to its base around her brow.

"Long live Elsyn the Priest-Queen," came a shout from somewhere in the room. Another person took it up, and another, until the entire room was shouting. "Long live Elsyn." "Long live the Priest-Queen." "May the god be with her." "May she rule justly."

Taryn wished she could stand next to her sister, that Elsyn could lean on her invisible self under the weight of the crown and the horns. But she couldn't imagine Elsyn would want her now, and she didn't think the illusion would hold up if she weren't tucked in a corner. She had wanted to talk to her, to explain, to ask questions, but Elsyn had made a point of never having a free moment when Taryn might get her alone.

The king had found her standing outside Elsyn's new rooms, now that she no longer lived in the temple dormitories, waiting for her to emerge into the hallway. He had interlaced his fingers with hers and looked down at her.

"Some things are best left to heal for a while before testing them," he had said. "You can come back here."

Now, Ash put their arm around her waist and led her away through a hidden door.

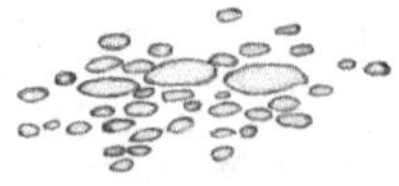

The three of them rode north, leaving Ildar with a group of mounted goblins. Lilith, annoyed that she not been able to take part in any of the violence, set a bruising pace, only slowing when Nel peeled off onto the shoulder of the road to stand panting and shivering, his hide dark with sweat. Ash dismounted immediately and walked with him for the next hour, clucking their tongue and producing bits of dry cheese and bread from their knapsack to feed to him.

They camped in a stretch of forested parkland. Taryn vaguely though there might be a grand house over at the end of the valley, someplace she had visited as part of a large retinue as a small child. Or perhaps not. She wondered if her memories would stop returning when she entered the goblin kingdom, or if they might fade away altogether.

Ash kept shooting her worried looks. They knelt by the firepit the king had dug, slicing a loaf of bread and toasting each piece in turn on a stick. They had produced a small round of fresh cheese, a lump of butter, and a tiny pot of honey from—where?—and were assembling somewhat less luxurious pieces of toast than usual.

Taryn, her side still numb, leaned against the king. He was very warm, and she was very tired. He rubbed his knuckles over her back, and she tried to focus on Ash's hands as they cut slices of cheese and smeared them on the bread. Her mind kept trying to wander away, thinking of Elsyn's frozen face under her crown, the other-Taryn's perfect copy of her own face, Oberon's face. But she —she was here. She was not in any of the places she had lost or had saved herself from. She was here, with two people she loved. It was not enough, maybe. It had not been fair. None of it had been fair.

"Are you all right?" the king asked, some time later, when the toast had been entirely consumed.

"No," Taryn said.

"Will you return with me?"

And be his queen, Taryn thought. Her heart hurt. She did not know how to answer him. What about Ash? she wanted to say. Will Ash come too?

"Ash," she said. "Why do you have a changeling mark?"

Both the witch and the goblin king went very still.

"You're not a fairy," she went on. "You're human, or you were. Why do you have the star? The other—*she* had it too."

"Well." Ash stood up from where they had been kneeling by

the fire, as though they might go do some chore at the edge of the camp, but instead of walking away they just stood there, staring at the trees as if they could provide an answer.

"Oberon is very old," the goblin king said. "Older than me. Perhaps not older than my father."

"Certainly older than me," Ash said bitterly.

"He has been quiet, these last eleven years. He did not want to draw attention to what he was hiding. There would have been people who would have come for you, if they'd realized."

"They didn't," Taryn said.

"Even so. Before, Oberon went abroad more often. He had a hand in many tricks, many hoodwinks, many disasters, and he set many plots unrolling which he found—I suppose he found *amusing*. And many of the things he did, he did for the *amusement* of his daughter."

"There are some who only care to cause havoc, and whether one person or a thousand are involved does not matter," Ash said. They passed one hand over their face, and then came back to kneel in front of the two of them. "Many humans can recognize a changeling mark. At least, they did in the country where I was a child. A changeling in a normal family, where the child is bathed by their parents, where they play outside and go swimming, would not go unnoticed for long."

"But you're not a changeling," Taryn said. Her heart felt like it was trying to crawl out of her chest.

"What is true is less important than what people think is true," Ash said, and Taryn's heart fell the rest of the way out. "And a changeling is terrible luck to have on your farmstead. Curdles the milk, makes the cheese go rotten, all of that. They were afraid of me, afraid of what I could do, afraid of what I could learn."

"Your cheese has never been rotten!" Taryn said helplessly.

"So I left," Ash went on, inexorably. "I left as soon as I was able and went off to find out where I'd really come from. My foster family had done their best to be kind, in spite of knowing I oughtn't have been there. I thought I could send back their real child to them, as a sort of repayment."

"And then," the king said, "you fell in service to the line of

Haldar."

"May all the gods bless and keep your mother, wherever she has gone," Ash responded, with a trace of their old smile. "Should we all be gifted to know someone so ferocious! . . . I fell in service. I have told you many of the stories of that time, Taryn. They were good years, and I didn't know how to get into a fairy hill, and I didn't want to even if I could. And then—"

Taryn crawled forward and laid her hands on Ash's knees. They looked startled and then grateful, lightly touching their fingertips to her knuckles.

"A young goblin was stolen and taken under Oberon's hill," they said. "And we went to rescue him, the pair of us." They nodded at the king, who bowed his head.

"Usually he's not such a fool as to take one of my kinsfolk. We are quick to take them back."

"The changeling and the child they replace cannot be in the same house," Ash said woodenly. "As you know now. We approached Oberon, his daughter seated at his right hand, and made our demands. He returned the young goblin. I asked for my human counterpart to be given to them, too, so they might deliver the child home, to their real family, and I would swear allegiance to the king under the hill."

Taryn wanted to knock Ash down and lie on top of them until she could press all the sadness out. "There wasn't another child. It was only the mark, for a game. To see if your fo — your real family would believe the trick."

"Yes," Ash said. They did not look at either Taryn or the king. "And then I went to hide in the wood for eleven years, because I was ashamed that I had believed it, too."

"And Oberon," the goblin king said, "decided he had better hide the *daughter* who had asked him to play such a game, such an amusing bit of fun—"

"In the safest place he could think of," Ash said. "A royal palace, backed by a great temple."

"Why hide her? Why—"

"Because," the king said softly, "I made a vow under the hill, to take his daughter from him and make her my queen—and then to

119

destroy his daughter utterly."

Taryn turned to stare at him, and he stared back at her with his very many-hued eyes.

"In just those words," she said finally.

"In those words."

It was as she had suspected in the throne room. He had kept the letter of the vow, she thought. A daughter and a foster daughter are all the same in the eyes of magic. But Oberon—Oberon had not known he would keep it in this way. As far as he knew, he was stealing a sacrifice for the goblin king, so his daughter could go on having her fun, destroying things and people.

She lifted her hands from Ash's knees and pressed them to her face.

"My beloveds," the king said, his deep voice very soft. "I am sorry."

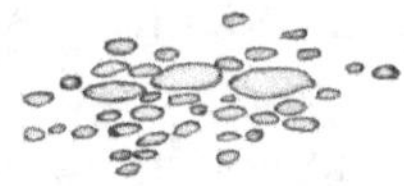

The next morning Ash was gone. The bottomless knapsack was tucked under Taryn's elbow. Nel trotted around the camp and whinnied in the most forlorn of voices.

"They've gone back to the wood," the goblin king said.

"What is the fastest way there?" Taryn said, and he hesitated.

"If they do not wish us to follow—"

"If they do not wish us to follow, it is because they are telling themself a great number of lies," she said irately.

"Perhaps Ash thinks you would rather not see them, now that you know the truth," he said. His eyes moved over her face.

"That's the most foolish thing I've ever heard," Taryn said. That was probably exactly what Ash had thought, she realized, her heart clenching. "You've known the truth for years, and you never wanted them to leave."

"No," he said. "But they did not believe me either."

"What is the fastest way to the wood?"

"There are many ways into that wood," he said evenly. "But

I only know one."

Taryn stood with her hands on her hips and stared at him. "What will happen to me if I pass through your kingdom?"

"You have taken vows," he said. "But if you turn away now, the magic may not catch you, or it may not catch you for many years. You were only in my home for a short time; it does not know you so well as it knows me. You might find another way to Ash."

The goblin king still wore the black clothes he had been given for the coronation. His appearance remained mostly human, though his ears were long and his eyes very sharp. He looked away from her, as though he could not control his expression.

Taryn thought of following Ash up to the pasture, of carrying empty buckets up the path and buckets filled with milk back down it. She thought of weeding. She thought of cattle, both sacred and profane, and of wicked goats and horses. Lilith, whose pride would not allow her to mope, was busily wrenching up small trees by their roots and trampling them around the edge of the camp.

She thought of Elsyn, standing alone on the dais in the throne room, surrounded by hundreds of faces. She thought of the goblin king in his castle, with Ildar and Kandar and the dozens of cousins who would draw their swords or raise their spears for him. She thought of her things spread out over the floor of the king's tent as she worked steadily on new magics. She had been raised to be a queen, and she had been made a witch.

She thought of holding Ash in the loft and of lying beneath the king. She thought of being pressed between them both in the bed in the wizard's inn.

She thought of the vows taking hold of her as she spoke them in the castle, surrounded by goblins. That lacing to the ground and to the past had felt permanent, steadfast. She did not think the vows would leave her be for long, though possibly she could seek help to break them.

What do I want? she thought. What do I deserve, given all that I have done and all that has been done to me?

He wants to give me a choice, she realized. But I've already made my choices.

Taryn walked close to the king. He kept his head turned away, but she could see his eyes glinting as he looked back at her.

Silently she wound her hands in his tunic and pulled downward. He knelt without resisting, and she let her hands slide over his chest. He was tall enough that even on his knees, his face was level with her throat.

Taryn rested her arms on his shoulders. "We are going to go back to your castle together and take the sure way to the wood," she said into his ear. "And then we will find Ash."

"And then?" the king asked, his voice a whisper of air against her throat.

"And then we will hope."

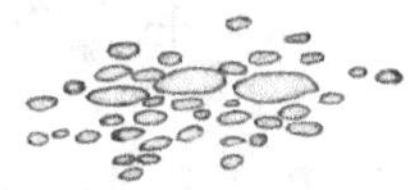

When they returned to the castle the goblins and the horses were celebrating. There was a great deal of raucous singing and frolicking around the bailey, hooves striking sparks against stones. A great tun of some strange bubbly drink had been opened and a bonfire built next to it.

Nel and Lilith remembered how tired and put-upon they both were upon entering the gate and, after several pairs of inebriated hands had shucked the saddles off them, went immediately to roll in the wallow that the herd had dug out at the far end of the line of tents. The king murmured something to one of the cousins—Taryn thought she heard the word "alfalfa"—and then turned to her with a wry look on his face. "Shall we walk out on the moor road? Or wait until morning?"

Taryn opened her mouth to say that she could not bear to wait when a curious motion caught the corner of her eye.

She turned, and there, silhouetted in front of the bonfire, was a flat dark shape, fluttering in the breeze like a bit of paper.

The illusion seemed to know that she'd seen it and skimmed away from the fire and back toward the great hall.

"What—"

"*Look,*" she said, seizing the king's hand. "Follow me."

The shadow flipped away from them, sliding through the entrance arch. Someone had left one of the great doors ajar, and it curvetted through the gap.

The great hall was very still. The bonfire was high enough outside to mask the shadows thrown by the moonlight, but in here, the floor was awash in a pale glow. The shrine to the ancestors of the king's mother rose in the center, dark, foreboding in its darkness.

The illusion flopped around on the second tier of figures, threading itself between carvings, some of them still splintered. Taryn watched it intently.

"I am sorry," she said, her voice very soft among the echoes in the stone.

"For what?" the king asked, sounding sarcastic and sad.

"For breaking something that holds a memory of your family," she said.

He was quiet for a minute. "I am sorry for not finding a way to explain what I meant to do—and what part you were to play in it."

Taryn considered his words. "That isn't enough."

"No," he agreed. He shot her a sharp look. "But I suspect you will tell me when you decide what is."

The shadow freed itself from the shrine and dove to the floor, where it skimmed the flagstones until it met a wall and turned, shimmering, to swim off again. Then it stopped, suddenly, hovering.

"What do you want to show us?" Taryn murmured as she knelt. The illusion had paused over a misshapen stone, a shadowy dent forming a sort of mouth in one end.

"*Ah,*" the king breathed.

He knelt too, put his hand into the mouth of the stone, and lifted.

The illusion whistled through the dark opening and disappeared. Taryn whispered the light charm and caught the little orb as it fell from her lips. Stairs wound away below them.

"This is one of the ways to my father's hearth," the goblin king said. "I have not opened any of them in many years."

Taryn held the orb deeper into the dark space. The illusion flapped itself once at the very edge of the light the charm cast and then was gone again.

They descended the stair into the depths beneath the castle. Taryn went first, one hand tracing the uneven rocks of the passage, one holding the charm in front of her. The king followed close behind, one hand fisted in the back of her tunic. When the light faded away, Taryn murmured a new one.

The stairs went down for a very long time. It was cold underground, and Taryn thought she could hear the echoing of water dripping and rushing all around her. Periodically they passed a split in the rock that let a cold gust of air rush across their faces.

The downward passage let them out into a tight hall with many passages branching off it. Taryn lifted her light, and the flat, papery illusion unpeeled itself from a stone wall and flew through one of the passage openings. They followed and kept following.

They stopped once, when a charm just emerging from her lips illuminated a great face pressed against the floor with a tremendous arm thrown over it, both extending from a gargantuan back that arched upward and pressed against the ceiling. When Taryn spoke more lights into existence, they clung round the face and showed it to be a great, stony goblin, deeply asleep, skin gray in profound slumber.

"Do you know them?" she whispered to the king.

He nodded but said nothing. They continued onward.

The hall that the illusion led them down started to rise into a gradual slope. It also narrowed; soon Taryn had turned sideways, and the king had hunched himself downward, as they crept forward between bulky stones that partially blocked the way. The light charm could only illuminate a short distance in front of them in this part of the passage. She slid on a wet patch on the floor and knocked into one, yelping. The king grabbed her before she could fall, and Taryn stood pressed against him for a moment before something clicked into her brain.

"That sounded *hollow*," she said out loud, reaching out her hand. She rapped her knuckles against what she had taken for a stone, and it thudded. It didn't feel like rock; it felt like wood. She drew her fingers across its surface; it was round and constructed of individual planks. She called the light to her, and it showed her again what she had felt.

"It's a barrel," she said, puzzled.

The king touched her elbow and pointed over her shoulder.

The barrel was jammed together with dozens of crocks in a narrow space. They were under a sort of overhang that made the space very dark, but just ahead she could see where it opened into a bigger room. A square of moonlight lay on the floor. They were no longer deep underground, but where were they?

The king breathed in deeply through his nose, and Taryn mimicked him unconsciously.

"*Oh*," she whispered.

"You had better not be rats," came Ash's voice from on top of the loft. "I absolutely refuse to have rats in my house."

The illusion flipped past them and fluttered upward in the moonlight insouciantly. Taryn and the king threaded their way past Ash's barrels and crocks.

They emerged when the witch had climbed halfway down the ladder. They twisted to stare at the king and the queen. The three of them blinked at each other. Ash's mouth fell slightly open.

"You—you—"

"And you," Taryn said.

"Oh, love," Ash said and finished coming down the ladder.

They stood together in the dark cottage. Ash reached out a hand as though they would touch Taryn's cheek, only to pull it back suddenly.

"I'm sorry," they said finally. "I had forgotten—it's been too long since I was among people. I can't—it's too much for me, these days. I've only had to keep the cows and the goats and the pigs happy for ten years—and none of them know anything—or really have the capacity to be embarrassed at all, to tell the truth—I don't have to explain myself, and I've lost the knack of explaining anyway—"

"What about me?" Taryn asked. "I'm people. You were among me—rather, with me, for several weeks—"

"That's not the same," Ash said, sounding a bit cross. "You

didn't ask me for anything."

"I asked you for *many* things," Taryn said softly.

Ash hesitated. "Well, nothing that I didn't want to give." They looked over Taryn's shoulder, at the king. "And you—you at least know that I am—I am unreliable."

"I know no such thing," the king said.

"I left for *eleven years*," they said. "*You* would never do that."

"I have never had everything I knew about myself proved to be a lie," the king said, looking from Ash to Taryn.

"No," Ash said slowly. "But even so—"

"Even so *nothing*," Taryn burst out. "I love you and I don't want to lose you. I *choose* you—both of you. You belong to me. I've already lost more than anyone had any right to ask me to give." She cleared her throat and blinked her eyes very quickly. "I'll come to the wood every *day*, if you can't stand to live among the cousins, but I will see you. I will." She stopped, feeling suddenly out of breath. She felt the king rest his hands on her back, reassuring.

Ash seemed entirely lost for words.

"I've taken vows to my king, and I will take vows to you too," Taryn went on.

"I won't bind you to me," the witch said. "I won't bind anyone."

"We are, both of us, already bound," the king said, his voice both amused and sad. "By love and by trust, if not by magic."

Ash was silent for a long time. When they finally spoke, their voice shook. "You must understand that it is—it is not an easy thing, to have the whole world offered up to you."

They seized Taryn suddenly in a hard hug, pressing their face into her shoulder, and then turned to the king. The hug became tighter and more complicated, and Taryn bent her head to kiss one face and stretched upward to kiss the other.

Acknowledgments

(from Juniper)

I give my regards to the sea.

To my neighbor, the Goat-Farmer On A Cliff, I say: I paid you for a pound of butter and four pounds of cheese two weeks ago, so where is it?

Acknowledgments

(from Sharon)

I am deeply obliged to Theodore Coffin, M.E.D., and Arden Powell, who beta-read *The Changeling* and offered many helpful suggestions. Thanks also to the friends and family who greeted news of this novella project with enthusiasm.

It has been an odd moment to write and produce a gentle novella, moving straight from seasonal depression into the anxiety accompanying a global pandemic, and yet, perhaps it is as good a moment for tenderness as any.

About the author

Juniper Butterworth is an elderly goblin who lives by the sea and eats cheese, bearing only a passing resemblance to Sharon J. Gochenour, a writer and illustrator living in Massachusetts. Between the two of them, they've visited a few places and consumed a few dairy products.

Links to more writing, artwork, blogging, and news can be found on sharonjgochenour.com.

A preview of the next book of the Goblins and Cheese sequence

Priest-Queen

Elsyn was pretending she couldn't see the goblin perched in the tree.

Of the twenty-two sacred cows kept by the high temple, six were currently in milk. Pumpkin had twin bull calves and was perfectly happy. Cabbage and Parsnip each had an exceedingly large heifer calf. But Squash and Onion, both prodigious milkers, had produced puny offspring this spring, who could barely empty half their udders. Turnip's calf had been stillborn—harbinger of the awful things the year was to bring, Elsyn thought grimly. So twice daily, Elsyn took out the milking stool and a bucket and herded the milkers into the southern paddock. She took a small bag of oats to reward the three who didn't need her for letting her check their teats for redness and their milk for lumps.

Five years ago, they temple had kept at least a hundred cattle, but that didn't bear thinking about.

The goblin had folded himself into the branches of a

gnarled pine that grew on top of one of the many hillocks that rumpled the holy pasture. He was dark and wearing dark clothing, so perhaps he thought he would pass for a shadow, pressed against the trunk of the tree.

The tufted tail is rather noticeable, Elsyn thought. Besides that, he was a huge creature and didn't fold to a particularly compact size. Perhaps he wasn't used to going among humans.

She wasn't quite used to having goblins in the palace yet. There had been a small contingent left behind after the coronation three weeks ago, but a second, larger group had just arrived the previous night. This fellow was one of the second party.

Elsyn finished with Squash and turned to Onion, shoving a calf's nose away from the bucket.

The goblin had crept out along a branch and was peering down toward her when she next caught a glimpse of him out of the corner of her eye. She took the stool and moved it to Turnip, who shifted and sighed with relief when she started to milk.

"Poor old girl," she muttered, thumping the cow's side affectionately. Turnip had been trying to steal one of Pumpkin's calves since spring, and Pumpkin was having none of it.

When her udder was empty, Elsyn flipped the hinged lid down on the bucket, tucked the stool under her arm, and before she could lose her nerve, strode toward the pine tree.

"Good day to you," she called upward. "Do you need help?"

The goblin didn't move.

"I hope you aren't hiding," Elsyn said, annoyed. "Because I can see you perfectly well."

After a minute the goblin slid down to a lower branch and bent his face toward hers.

It was a startling face, dominated by a pair of enormous golden eyes, shot through with amber and orange. He looked human but not quite. His nose was an odd shape, and the two tusks protruding from his lower jaw gave his mouth a surly twist. This close, she could see a layer of fine, dark fur covered his skin. His ears were large and pointed, almost cat-like, and the fur on his face rose into a stiff black crest on the top of his skull. The overall effect was handsome but startling.

He balanced on the branch like an acrobat or a leopard, claws on his feet and his hands digging into the bark, his tail held out stiff behind him for balance.

"Sir?" she prompted, when he said nothing.

"When did you learn to milk cows?" the goblin asked in a gravelly baritone.

"I suppose I was thirteen," Elsyn said, flinching a bit at the memory of that year. If this year had been bad, that one had been infinitely worse.

"They listen to you," he said, jerking his chin at Turnip, who had followed Elsyn, lowing mournfully.

"All the priests of the Two-Being God can speak to cattle."

"Yes, but they *listen* to you," he repeated. "That big calf could have had the milk out of your bucket ten times, if she'd wanted to."

Elsyn felt her cheeks get warm. "Yes, I suppose you're right."

"Can you speak with other animals as well, or just cows?"

"Only cows, so far as I know. The older priests told me that they could usually hear goats and deer, but I haven't had a chance to try." She felt at a conversational disadvantage with her hands full, so she set down the stool and put the bucket of milk on top of it and then put her hands on her hips. "Are you looking for someone in particular, or just hoping to speak with a priest generally? I don't mean to be rude, but there's barely anyone left in the high temple anymore, and it's not much to look at, if you're wanting to sight-see. We haven't had a high priest since the winter before last." She hesitated, before adding, "The last decade has not been kind."

"No one in particular," the goblin said. "Just wandering around."

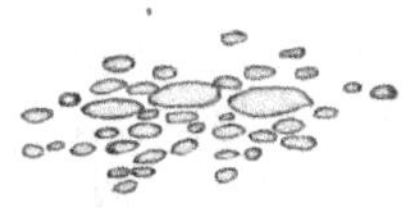

Kandar had been looking for Elsyn Ardloch, newly-crowned queen of this human country that ran from the mountains in the north and west, to the high steppes in the east, and down to the sea in the south. Most significantly, it was the country that the goblin road ran into, when it descended from the slightly out-of-register goblin mountains that were just up and to the left of the other range in the north.

He had only a very vague idea of what human queens occupied themselves with, but he did not think it generally included milking cows. He had been told, of course, that Elsyn was a Priest-Queen—the very first in all this realm's history—but somehow his imagination had not stretched to the daily responsibilities of the holy order. Milking seemed like the sort of thing that a person might delegate, once she'd been crowned.

Kandar had been sent south by his cousin the goblin king, who he loved steadfastly, in service of his queen Taryn, who Kandar despised. Taryn had spent eleven years under a fairy hill and had correspondingly off-putting habits. She had become something less, or something more, than human during those years, delicately picking her way through fairy magic and fairy politics, being transformed or enchanted on the daily whims of Oberon, the fairy king. Kandar found her itchy on his better days and domineering on her worst.

He had—fairly naturally, he thought—assumed that her younger sister would be rather like her. It was this assumption that had led him to climb a tree in the paddock where another priest had assured him the young queen was usually to be found in the afternoons. He thought he would learn a great deal about her very quickly when she noticed him.

He might have, but his thoughts became jumbled when Elsyn came over the next hillock, leading a small group of cows. She looked a bit like Taryn, in the sense that a destrier resembles a palfrey; they both had a great mass of black hair, dark brows over great dark eyes, and arched noses. Elsyn, however, was a head taller than her sister, with wide shoulders and wide hips under a priest's shift. Taryn had occasional bouts of delicacy, perhaps brought on by many years of restriction and vicious treatment under the fairy hill, but Elsyn looked to be her opposite: a great, powerful, fat woman, the sort of human who could carry a calf under each arm. Her face and shoulders were brown with the sun.

She noted him immediately but got on with milking. The cattle treated her as another cow, one who had oddly chosen to go upright on two legs. They licked her face and chatted with her in small grunts and moos. Each of the sacred cows was a massive beast, with a pair of curving horns that stretched as far above their heads as their backs were above the ground, each horn as big around as a sundial as its base. They observed him, too, with wary intelligence in their large eyes. Kandar suspected that if he made any impolite advances toward the queen, he would be skewered.

He did not think about anything more for a long while as he watched her intently, until she was standing under the tree, frowning up at him.

"Well," she said finally. "If you're not looking for anyone, perhaps you should come up to the cheesemaking room with me."

"I don't need anyone looking after me," Kandar said. His tail lashed once, involuntarily. That had sounded ruder than he had intended to be.

The corner of Elsyn's mouth tipped up. "No, I'm sure you don't, but if you surprise the bull or the boss cow when you're wandering around, they'll look after you a little less kindly than I will. Besides, there's probably some fresh cheeses that are ready to test."

She picked up the stool and the bucket of milk again and walked uphill, clearly assuming he would follow.